The Lion's
Paw

The Lion's Paw

by Robb White

illustrated by Ralph Ray

A.W. INK
PUBLISHING ROBB WHITE'S BOOKS
RIVERTON, UTAH 84065

for Rebe

Illustrations

"Here's a birthday present," Nick said stiffly. "I
made it all myself"   9

Penny took the mop out of the bucket and held it
ready to strike   21

Before Penny went below she asked, "Do you think
we got away, Ben?"   55

Slowly they warped the boat far up the narrowing
creek   71

"What's your name, son?" the man asked   89

Rushing toward him was an enormous alligator   165

"We've come a long way, haven't we, Ben," Penny
said in a low voice   177

"But watch out for a little snake with a blunt nose
and a sort of blunt tail," Ben said   191

All three of them searched the beach that day   197

The *Lion's Paw* caught the first huge wave right in
the teeth   215

The Lion's
Paw

ENNY tied the ribbon in a little
bow on top of her head and walked across to the window.
Standing there in her petticoat, she looked first down into
the place they called the courtyard. She always looked out
of her window this way—first down at the straight
graveled walks between the scraggly flower beds and thin
lawns. She would look at everything in the courtyard before she would let her eyes begin to follow the widest
walk. This one went straight away from the gray stone
buildings, and Penny would follow it slowly with her eyes.
If anyone was walking along it, or if the big boys were
working with wheelbarrows or raking the gravel, she
would not look at them. Instead she would pretend that
the walk was empty and that she, alone, was walking
along it, walking away from the buildings.

THE LION'S PAW

Penny followed the walk with her eyes until it came to the high iron gates. To her these gates were like a canyon, for they made the only break in the solid brick wall. The gates were nearly always closed, and they were closed now, so her eyes climbed up them until she saw the letters made of wrought iron which arched over the two tall gates. Penny always read the word backward because the sign faced away from the buildings.

E G A N A H P R O, she read. She and Nick, her brother, would never say that they lived in an orphanage. They lived in an eganahpro, and they weren't orphans; they were eganaps.

Penny made her eyes look at the sign for a long time before she would let them leap beyond it. She would look then straight over the trees and the road winding over to the town. She would ignore the huge oaks with Spanish moss hanging like dirty gray laundry from every limb. Her eyes would go swiftly beyond the town, beyond the church steeples sticking up above the green of the trees, until she could see the ocean.

As Penny looked at the sun on the sea now she thought, "I'm twelve years old today. This is my birthday and nobody knows it. Except, maybe, Nick. He might know it because I never forget his birthday and I always give him a present."

Then she thought, as a faraway breeze riffled the sunlight on the sea, "I bet I've looked at the sea a million times. When I first came here I couldn't see it because I was only four years old and they put me in the Baby House and I couldn't see anything but trees. But when I got to be six years old they gave me this room, and so for six years I've been looking out of this window at the ocean. Sometimes I've looked out of the window a hundred times in one day. I bet I've looked at it more than a million times."

The iron gates swinging open distracted her, and she watched a car coming slowly up the wide drive. It was a big, shiny car and she could look almost directly down on it when it stopped at the wide steps and the man and woman got out. Penny looked at them carefully and decided that they were nice. The lady had on a black dress with a red flower at her shoulder, and she had a little hat with another red flower on it. The man was tall and the toes of his shoes were very shiny. Soon they would come back to the car with one of the children from the Baby House. The car would drive out of the gates and the one from the Baby House would never come back through the gates again.

Penny looked across the courtyard at the rows of windows in the Boys' House. She knew exactly which one was Nick's, but the sun was behind the house now and his window was just a black rectangle in the gray wall. She wondered what Nick was doing, but he didn't come to the window, so at last Penny turned back into the bare little room and went on dressing.

When she was finished she stood in front of the small

3

mirror and looked at herself. Outside her window she heard the car's tires crunching on the gravel, but she didn't go over to watch it go out of the gates.

Whispering to her reflection in the mirror, Penny said, "I can't ever go out of those gates—not for good. Nick can go with that Mrs. Wertz if he wants to. He doesn't have to stay here. But nobody will ever adopt me."

But Nick did not like Mrs. Wertz. "She looks like a frog," Nick had said after the interview was over.

And Mrs. Wertz lived on a farm. She didn't live anywhere near the sea.

Penny felt the lump beginning to swell in her throat, and as she looked at her face in the mirror it began to get misty through the tears, and the red hair ribbon on top of her head became just a blotch of color and her wide-apart blue eyes were like pools of blue in her brown face.

Penny made herself stop crying because it was almost time for the bell. She wiped her eyes on the hem of her petticoat and blew her nose. Then she looked in the mirror again. She had a serious, wistful face, but when she smiled, as she made herself do now, the corners of her mouth curved upward, and her dark blue eyes seemed to have little lights in them. For the past month she had been assigned to the flower gardens, so her face was suntanned and her almost blond hair had been burned to a light gold color after days of working outdoors.

When the bell rang Penny joined the other children as they came streaming out of the various buildings. She

4

saw Nick come out of the Boys' House by himself and she waited for him under the water-oak tree.

Nick was only nine and a half, but he was bigger than some of the boys who were ten or even eleven. Penny watched him as he came toward her and thought how much like a grown-up man he looked. He wasn't scrawny —all legs and arms and joints—like most of the boys. He was compact; his shoulders were wide and his hips small, and he seemed to be all in one piece, not with one arm swinging off one way, the other another, and his legs wandering around.

Anyone could tell they were brother and sister because Nick had the same wide-set blue eyes and the same firm big mouth with upturning corners and the same wistfulness. His hair was more sandy-colored than Penny's, and his face was rounder.

" 'Lo," he said when he got to the tree.

" 'Lo."

"You still in the flower garden?" Nick asked.

Penny nodded.

"They assigned me to the kitchen for another month," Nick said angrily. Then he paused and said in a low whisper, "Just for that I'm going to run away."

"How?" Penny asked. She wasn't very interested because the eganaps all said they'd run away, but whenever one actually did he was always caught in a little while and brought back in disgrace.

Nick looked all around and came closer to her. "I've got it all planned."

5

THE LION'S PAW

Penny shook her head slowly. "They'll catch you and you'll have to walk the courtyard for a month—maybe more."

"They won't catch me," Nick said angrily.

Penny shrugged. "Anybody can run away. Only there's no place to run away to where they can't find you. You remember Pansy Brown who used to live on my floor? She ran away one time when we were marching to the movies. She tried to sleep under the porch of a house, and a lot of goats came under there too. Then it rained on her. And they caught her the next morning and made her come back. She caught a terrible cold and was in the dispensary for a long time. And after she got out she had to walk the courtyard just the same."

"I'm not going to sleep with any goats," Nick said. "I'm going to sea. I'm going to be a sailor. Go 'way away where they won't ever find me."

Penny looked toward the sea, but she couldn't see it when she was down in the courtyard. She sat down with her back against the tree, and Nick sat down beside her.

"I wish I could be a sailor," Penny said quietly. "I'd like it."

"I'm going to be," Nick said. "I'm not going to work in that old kitchen all my life."

Penny hardly heard him. "I bet I've looked at the ocean a million times," she said.

"I can't even see it," Nick said. "All I see out of my window is the Girls' House and some trees. I tried to swap

6

rooms with Melonhead because he doesn't like to look at it, but they wouldn't let me."

"I remember," Penny said. "Yesterday a big sailboat came in. The sails were so white."

"If I could get on a sailboat they couldn't ever find me, could they, Penny?" he asked.

"Nick," Penny said sternly, "you forget about running away, hear? There's no use even trying to."

Nick scowled at her. "If I stay here with you I'll have to work in the kitchen all the time. I won't even get out in the courtyard any more."

Penny felt the lump rising in her throat as she said slowly, "You can go with that Mrs. Wertz, Nick. She wants to adopt you."

"That's what I'm going to do," Nick said calmly. "But I'm not going to be adopted by that old woman. She hasn't got any colors in her eyes."

"If you go you have to be," Penny said, amazed.

Nick shook his head firmly. "No, they said I could go on a two-week tryout, and if Mrs. Wertz doesn't like me she can bring me back. Only," Nick said, his voice dropping to a whisper, "I'm going to run away from her before then."

Penny stared at her little brother, and Nick scowled harder.

"It isn't like running away from here," he said. "It's different when you run away before you've even been adopted. Isn't it different, Penny?"

7

"I guess so," Penny said slowly. "If somebody doesn't love you I guess it's all right to run away from them."

"That'll give me a head start," Nick said, excitement rising in his voice. "Nobody here will know I'm gone for a long time."

Penny looked at her brother in amazement. "Are you *really* going to, Nick?" she asked.

"I said I was," Nick said, his voice a little angry. "I'm getting older every day and I want to be a sailor." Then he hesitated a moment and in a different voice asked, "You think I ought to, Penny?"

"I don't know, Nick. It's awful dangerous. It scares me just to think of it."

"Me *too!*" Nick said, his voice low. Then he added loudly, "But I'm going to do it!"

Penny leaned back against the tree and thought of the whole wide world outside those iron gates. She had never felt as sad as this in all her life.

In a whisper Penny said, "I'll miss you, Nick."

Nick turned his head away. "Don't blubber," he said.

Penny stiffened. "I'm not blubbering. I was just being —polite."

Suddenly Nick dug down into his pants pocket and then held his hand out toward her, the fingers tightly closed.

"Here's a birthday present," he said stiffly. "I made it all by myself." He opened his fingers over her hand. "I've been working on it for more than a month."

8

"HERE'S A BIRTHDAY PRESENT," NICK SAID
STIFFLY. "I MADE IT ALL MYSELF."

THE LION'S PAW

He dropped into Penny's hand a little heart-shaped piece of gray limestone. At the V of the heart there was a hole with a piece of white string strung through it.

"You can wear it around your neck if you want to," Nick said.

Penny turned the little heart over and saw her initials scratched into the soft gray stone. "P. B."—Penelope Brown.

"It's beautiful, Nick," she said softly. "It's the beautifullest thing I ever saw."

"It's just a piece of rock," Nick said.

"But it's a heart." Penny put the string around her neck and turned the stone over so the initials were outside. "I'll wear it all my life," she said, holding it in her hand.

"When I get rich I'll get a gold chain for it," Nick said. "When I get to be a sailor I'll go to India or Africa or someplace and get a gold chain and bring it back to you."

Penny let the little heart go and felt it lying against her throat. "Nick," she said, almost whispering, "I'll go with you."

Nick turned to look at her. "You mean—now?"

Penny nodded.

"Run away?" Nick asked slowly.

She nodded again.

"From here?"

"Yes."

THE LION'S PAW

"When I run away?" He was whispering.

"Yes. You sneak back here and open the gates. They open from the outside. Then we'll run away together," Penny said.

"All right," Nick said, his voice almost soundless.

Penny suddenly felt frightened at what they were going to do. Then she thought, "This is the last chance we'll ever have to get out of this place. No one else will ever want me, and Nick is getting older all the time. The nice people only want the little babies. If we don't go now when we've made up our minds to go we never will. We've got to go this time."

"All right," Penny said. "Let's go tell them you'll go on the tryout with Mrs. Wertz."

The high iron gates closed slowly behind the muddy pick-up truck, and Mrs. Wertz drove away with Nick sitting beside her on the hard, slippery seat. Nick looked back for a moment at the arched sign, but it looked different when it was spelled right—ORPHANAGE. It wasn't EGANAHPRO any more.

Then Mrs. Wertz took a fork in the road which led directly away from the sea. She hadn't said a word since she had started, but after she drove down the road for a while she suddenly said, "If we understand each other from the very beginning we'll have a happy little family."

Nick nodded.

"I believe in hard work and plenty of it," Mrs. Wertz

said. "And when the work is finished, then playtime."

Nick nodded again.

"You will have your own little tasks to do each day," Mrs. Wertz said. "I don't believe in going around haphazardly. And each little task must be done and done right before you go on to the next. On my little farm there's plenty of work for all—cows to be fed and milked, chickens and ducks, the table garden, and of course keeping the house neat and clean, and keeping the barn sanitary. If the little hands are kept occupied, then they don't get into trouble."

Nick slowly turned his head so that he could look back down the road toward the ocean. But he couldn't see it and he waited, hoping that they would come to an open place where the trees wouldn't be in the way.

"Are you listening to me, Nicholas?" Mrs. Wertz asked.

Nick jerked his head around. "Yes, ma'am," he said.

"When I speak to you you must always listen," Mrs. Wertz said. "Pay careful attention."

"Yes, ma'am," Nick said.

They passed another fork in the road, and Nick read the names on the pointing arrows. Then he thought, "I won't have any trouble finding the way back. All I have to do is go toward where the sun is and I'll come to the orphanage after a while." He wondered if it would be hard to get the gates open so Penny could slip out.

The truck rattled on down the road.

Chapter 2

EHIND them in the night-dark town a clock struck two. The sudden sound of it startled Penny and Nick, and they walked closer together, their swinging arms touching every now and then.

Thinking back over the hours which had passed, Penny could remember only a few of the things, for most of the memory seemed to be just walking. But it had been so easy. She had pretended to be working in the flower beds near the high gates. Nick had come, opened the gates, and she had slipped out. That was all. They had run until they couldn't breathe any more, then had hidden in some bushes to wait for nightfall. Then they had walked. Hour after hour they had walked toward the sea.

Nick was beginning to lag a little, she noticed, and finally he said, "I'm sleepy, I think."

14

"I am too," Penny said. "But we'll find a boat we like soon."

"I never have been up until two o'clock in the morning," Nick said. "Everything's different, isn't it?"

Penny had noticed that. As they walked along the wharves the ocean didn't seem to be the same one she had looked at from her window. Now it was black-dark beyond the pale wood of the wharves, and it made a soft, slushing noise under where they were walking. It wasn't shiny and clean-looking any more. It didn't seem to be very friendly.

Moored to the wharves were all sorts of boats, but they were dark and dirty-looking and weren't sailboats. They made creaking noises as they bumped and rubbed against the pilings, and the water made little slapping sounds under their sterns. None of them looked like the beautiful sailboat Penny had seen coming into the harbor.

They were almost to the end of the wharves when Nick said, "There's a tall pole." It was the mast of a sailboat, and when they got to it they both knew that they had found what they wanted.

The sailboat wasn't gloomy-looking like the others. The hull was painted white so that it seemed to gleam above the black water; the woodwork around the deck was varnished so that it shone even at night, and there were bright metal things on it. For a long time Penny and Nick stood on the wharf just looking down at the sailboat. Then, without saying anything, Penny jumped lightly

15

down on the deck and held up her hand to help Nick. But he wouldn't take her hand as he jumped down beside her. As they walked along the deck, though, he took her hand.

Back at the end of the boat there was a deep cockpit, but the door leading into the inside of the boat was locked. Penny knocked on it—the sound of her knuckles very loud in the quiet night—but nothing happened.

"I guess the people aren't in there," Penny whispered.

Nick sat down on the cushions in the cockpit. "I could go to sleep right here," he said.

"People would see us—in the morning," Penny said. She looked up at the bare wharf and then along the deck of the boat. Up near the mast there was a long white roll of something, and she climbed out of the cockpit and unrolled it across the deck. It was the suit of sails for the boat, light canvas which smelled like new rope and resin.

Penny tiptoed back to where Nick was still sitting on the cushions. "I've found a place. And it's got covers and everything. Come on."

Nick climbed up beside her, and they went and lay down on a fold of the sails and pulled the other folds over them like a blanket. For a moment they lay still, both on their backs, looking straight up at the stars in the dark sky. Then Nick snuggled up against her.

"Smells good, doesn't it?" Nick said.

"Yeah," Penny said softly. She breathed in a lungful of air, smelling the tar and creosote of the wharves, the

16

smell of fish and salt water, the clean faint scent of the boat itself, and the ropy smell of the clean sails. "Wonderful," she said.

The boat rocked gently under them, and soon they began to feel the warmth of the sails and of each other. A star above them fell swiftly past the other stars.

"I hope the people who own this boat won't be mean," Nick said, his voice slow with sleepiness.

Penny put her arm under his head. "They won't be," she said. "Mean people wouldn't have a boat like this."

Soon Nick was sound asleep. Penny's arm felt numb where his head rested on it, but she didn't move it. "We've run away," she thought. "We've run away for good and are going to be sailors. We won't ever have to go back there. This boat will take us far away from them."

Then she thought, "I'll stay awake all night so that if they come looking for us I'll hear them and can wake up Nick in time for us to hide. I'll just lie here and look at the stars and smell all the smells and listen to the little noises and I won't go to sleep at all."

And in a moment she was sound asleep with Nick's head cradled on her shoulder and the stars shining down on her face.

The next thing Penny knew, water was falling on her forehead drop by drop. In her sleep she turned her head from side to side, but the water still dropped on her forehead and at last she woke up.

17

THE LION'S PAW

It was full daylight. A foot above her face there was a gray stringed mop, and even as she lay looking up at it a silver drop of water fell from the end of one of the strings and hit her squarely in the eye.

Penny sat up, avoiding the mop, and when she did Nick's head rolled off her arm and thumped on the deck and he woke up, yelling "Ouch!"

Holding the mop over her head was a boy wearing white sailor pants rolled to his knees. He was barefooted and bare-chested and was standing with his legs apart, still letting the mop drip on Penny's head. He was much bigger than Penny, and his skin was sunburned until it was as brown as the mahogany table in the reception room.

"Stop," Penny said, trying to get out from under the mop. Nick sat up and stared at the boy.

He at last swung the mop away and set it down in a bucket. Then, still with his legs apart, he put his hands on his hips and said, "What are you doing on my boat? Rumpling up the sails and everything."

"Nothing," Penny said.

"Just sleeping a little," Nick said.

The boy looked angry. He had a lot of freckles on his face, a stubby nose, and grayish-green eyes. His hair was cut so short all over his head that it stood straight up. Penny looked at his face and then at how tall he was and how broad-shouldered. His arms had a lot of muscles, she noticed, and his hands looked hard. It wouldn't be

18

any use trying to fight him, she decided. Even if she and Nick used all the tricks of fighting they had learned in the eganahpro, this boy could probably beat them up.

"Don't you know it's against the law to go on people's boats?" he demanded.

Nick solemnly shook his head.

"Is this your boat?" Penny asked. "All your own boat?"

The boy didn't answer for a moment and he looked away when he said, "It's my father's. But that doesn't make any difference." He got angry again and glared down at Penny. "As far as you coming aboard and rumpling up the sails and everything, it's my boat and you had no business aboard her."

"We didn't mean to," Penny said softly. "We really didn't. It was just late at night and we were tired. We looked at all the boats, and this one was the only nice one."

The boy suddenly sniffed the air, then turned around and ran forward. Even as he ran he seemed to disappear straight down through the deck. Nick stared at where he had been and said, whispering, "Where'd he go? Did he fall off?"

Penny stood up and saw that there was a little square hole in the deck forward of the mast. "He went down that hole," she said, also whispering.

"Maybe he went after a weapon," Nick said, getting up and standing behind her. "He looked awful mad."

Penny took the mop out of the bucket and held it

ready to strike, the mop end in her hand, as she advanced toward the hole. Nick crept silently beside her, his fists up and ready.

"Wallop him as soon as he sticks his head up," Nick whispered.

"And if that doesn't do it, you tackle him and I'll wallop him again," Penny said.

They got to the hole in the deck and stood ready, opposite each other.

"He's mighty big," Nick said a little dubiously.

Penny nodded, taking a better grip on the mop. "But I think he's going to tell on us. Maybe tell a policeman."

"Maybe we could talk him out of it if he would listen for a little while," Nick said.

Before Penny could answer the boy appeared on deck behind them. "Put that swab down," he yelled at Penny.

Penny whirled around. "Th-th-this?" she said, her tongue dry in her mouth, as she held out the mop.

"Put it in the bucket," the boy said. He walked up to Penny and glared down at her, his gray eyes flashing. "What were you going to do, swat me with that swab?"

"Oh no!" Penny said.

"No," Nick said.

The boy took the mop out of Penny's limp hands and stood it up in the bucket. "If you weren't a girl I'd take you by the seat of the pants and throw you in the bay," he said. He walked slowly away from them, his back to them, and sat down on the little dinghy turned upside

PENNY TOOK THE MOP OUT OF THE BUCKET
AND HELD IT READY TO STRIKE.

down across the cabin house. Then he looked at them for a moment. "Sails all rumpled," he said slowly. "Breakfast burned up. Deck not swabbed down. The whole day ruined. Why don't I just forget you're a girl and throw you in the bay anyhow? . . . Think I'll do it." He stood up again.

Penny held up her hand. "Wait a minute. Please, wait just a minute," she said, backing away until she bumped against something.

"You better not try," Nick said.

The boy sat down on the dinghy again. "Both of you go on home," he said. "Get off my boat and go on home. And don't ever come back."

Penny felt the lump pressing in her throat again. She looked up and down the beautiful boat and then she looked at the boy's face. His mouth didn't seem to be as angry-looking, and his eyes were a deeper gray than they had been. He didn't look like a mean boy.

But if she told him where they had come from all he would have to do would be to tell a policeman, or anybody, and she and Nick would have to go back to the gray buildings and the graveled courtyard. She thought of her bare, empty little room with one window, one bed, one chair.

Penny's whole heart was begging as she said softly, "We haven't got any."

"Any what?" the boy said.

"Home," Penny said.

23

"No home," Nick said, and sounded as though he were going to cry, but she knew he wouldn't.

"Everybody's got a home," the boy said.

Penny shook her head slowly. "Not everybody," she said.

"Everybody's got to live somewhere," he said.

Then Nick said suddenly, looking straight at the boy, "You're a dope."

Penny held her breath as the boy looked at Nick. He started looking at Nick's head, then he looked all the way down to Nick's feet and back up again. Then the boy looked at Penny. "Tough little character, isn't he?" the boy said quietly. "Who is he?"

Penny let her breath out slowly. "He's my brother. His name's Nick and mine's Penny."

The boy got up slowly and walked over to Nick. Nick stood his ground as the boy squatted on his haunches so their eyes were on the same level. The gray-green ones looked straight into Nick's wide blue ones, and Nick looked straight back, his head pushed forward a little.

"Now, son," the boy said, "what did you say?"

Penny saw Nick swallow before he answered: "I said, 'You're a dope.' And I'm not your son."

The boy rocked back and forth a little on his heels.

"Why?" he demanded suddenly.

"Because," Nick said, "we're eganaps, and eganaps don't have any homes; they live in eganahpros."

The boy got up and walked back to sit down on the

dinghy again. He looked at Nick for a long time, then he said, "What's an eganap?"

"An eganap hasn't got any father or mother," Nick said.

Penny said, "Nick! Sssssh!" And Nick looked at her and said, "I don't care, Penny. Let him tell on us if he wants to. He's just a dope anyway."

"Eganap," the boy said. "You mean 'orphan.'"

"Eganap," Nick said.

"It's a word we made up," Penny said. "It isn't a real word."

The boy looked at her slowly, and she noticed that the gray in his eyes was almost dark now. "I'm almost an eganap too," he said quietly.

Penny stared at him. "You mean your father and mother are dead? You mean you've run away too?"

The boy suddenly stood up. "We won't discuss it," he said. "Come on, before my breakfast burns again." Then he made a shrill whistling noise and said in a loud voice, "Clear the mess decks. Chow down!" He looked over his shoulder at Penny and said, "My father used to say that."

They had finished breakfast. Nick and Penny had washed all the dishes and put them back up in the little racks around the bulkheads. Nick had cleaned the frying pan and even shined the brass fittings on the little stove. Once, while the boy was out in the main cabin doing something, Nick had whispered, "Do you think he will start sailing away when we get everything washed?" And Penny had whispered back, "I hope so."

Everything was spick and span when Penny and Nick came into the main cabin, where the boy was sitting at the narrow table looking at some big pale maps. Penny winked hopefully at Nick and waited until the boy looked up at them.

"Well, there's nothing else to do," the boy said.

"Are you going to sail away now?" Nick asked.

The boy looked at him for a long time and then said, "I never sail away." He said it sadly and looked back down at the maps. "All I ever do is look at the charts and pretend that I'm sailing. Here, you see. . . ." He pointed at a chart with the needle point of a pair of dividers. "We're passing buoy number 23 in the St. Lucie River. Going west. It's a flashing green every four seconds."

"You mean you just stay right here? All the time?" Penny asked.

The boy nodded. "They won't let me go anywhere. Not by myself. Sometimes, on Sunday afternoon, my uncle comes and we go sailing. Yeah, we really sail!" the boy said bitterly. "We sail around and around this little bay until it makes you dizzy. We never see a wave, never see any blue water. Just this muddy soup. And if a little breeze rises and the boat begins to heel my uncle gets scared and we run for home."

"But doesn't your father ever go anywhere?" Penny asked.

Without saying anything the boy got up and went over to a little desk which was fitted into the bulkhead. He unlocked the desk and brought back to the table a locked steel box. Still without saying anything he unlocked the box and pulled out a telegram. He handed it to Penny.

The telegram read:

Deeply regret to inform you that your father, Lieutenant Benjamin Rush Sturges, United States Naval Reserve, is missing in action after the sinking of his ship. . . .

There was a lot more to the telegram, but Penny didn't read it. "Is that your father?" she asked in a low voice.

The boy nodded.

"What does it mean by 'missing'?" Nick asked. "Does it mean that they can't find him?"

"They think he's dead," the boy said. "See?" He got a letter out of the box which had come from the Secretary of the Navy. It said that the boy's father had been missing for a year without any trace of his being found, so the Secretary of the Navy had declared that he was dead.

"How can he do that?" Penny asked. "Just because they can't find him they can't declare that he's dead, can they?"

"They think he is," the boy said. He took the telegram and the letter and put them carefully back into the box. Then he looked at Penny and Nick. "But I know he isn't," the boy said. "He wrote me a letter once and I've

27

always believed what it said." He reached into the box again and got out a folder full of letters. He found the one he wanted and spread it out on the table. "This is what my father said," the boy said quietly.

The letter started:

"DEAR SKIPPER:

"He called me 'Skipper' when he was away from the boat," the boy explained. "When he was here I called *him* 'Skipper.'"

"DEAR SKIPPER:
"I think I'm finally going to get into something interesting. Can't tell you much, but I feel sure that the Japoons aren't going to like it, and they're going to try to make it rough for us.

"Here's something I wish you'd remember, Skipper. There are four things the Navy Department can say about me: First that I've been wounded. If they say that, you can believe 'em. Second, that I've been killed. I wouldn't put too much faith in that because I have no intention of getting bumped off out here. So if they say that about me, wait a little while and I'll turn up. Third, that I've been taken prisoner. If that happens, it may take me a few months to escape. Fourth, that I'm missing. That's a tough one because this is a big ocean. It might take me as much as a year to get back to you. But I'll be back, so don't worry."

The boy stopped reading and looked up at them. "It's been more than a year now," he said quietly. "He ought

28

to be back soon. And I haven't done what he asked me to do."

"What did he want you to do?" Penny asked.

"Find a Lion's Paw," the boy said.

"A what?" Nick asked.

"A Lion's Paw."

"Wouldn't the lion need it?" Nick asked.

"It's a sea shell," the boy said. "That's just the name of it."

"Oh," Nick said. "I thought it was on a lion."

"I told him I'd do it," the boy said. "And I haven't."

"We'll help you," Penny said.

The boy looked up at her, then he slowly shook his head. "The only Lions' Paws in the world are far away from here," he said.

"Well . . ." Penny said. "Let's go where they are."

The boy shrugged his shoulders. "How?" he asked.

"In this boat," Penny said. "It's a good boat, isn't it?"

The boy scowled at her. "I already told you that they won't let me. I already told you that the only place I can go in the boat is just around the bay—on Sunday afternoons."

"Who's 'they'?" Penny asked.

"My aunt and uncle. I live with 'em," the boy said.

"Could they catch you?" Penny asked.

"Catch me? What do you mean, catch me?"

"If you ran away," Penny said quietly.

Chapter 3

PENNY and the boy looked at each other for a long time. Penny knew that he was thinking about what she had said, and as she waited for him to make up his mind she could feel excitement beginning to boil inside her. If he just nodded his head and said he would go, she thought, she and Nick would be safe. They would sail away and never come back. They would go to all the places she had read about in her schoolbooks. They would be happy, and no bells would ring to make them do things they didn't want to do, and there wouldn't be walls around them all the time. Penny got so excited she stopped breathing while she waited for the boy to say he would go.

The boy slowly shook his head. "No," he said.

Penny could feel tears beginning to burn in her eyes.

Nick, who had been waiting, too, seemed to crumple up as he sat down slowly on one of the bunks.

"Why not?" Penny asked.

"They would find me and take the boat away from me," the boy said. "Then I wouldn't have—anything. They did it once. They wouldn't let me go aboard for a month just because I went out sailing one afternoon by myself."

"Couldn't we go where they couldn't find you?" Penny asked.

"They'd find me," the boy said, his voice hopeless.

Ever since she and Nick had run with the gates behind them Penny had felt hope rising in her. A feeling of freedom had been all around her as they had walked toward the ocean. Hope and freedom had grown stronger and stronger as the long night reached out ahead of them. She remembered looking up at the free stars when they were wrapped in the sails. She remembered how it had felt while she and Nick were washing the breakfast dishes and thinking that the boat would sail away soon. Now it was all dying.

But Penny made up her mind. This boat *had* to take them away. It just *had* to.

"Please," she said softly. "We're running away too. People are already looking for us. If you go with us they won't ever find you. We'll help you. We're strong; we'll work all the time. We won't ever sleep or anything until we've sailed so far away nobody could find us."

31

THE LION'S PAW

The boy shook his head.

Penny felt frantic, and her lower lip was beginning to tremble a little. She watched the boy twisting the pair of dividers between his fingers. "Well," she said slowly, "if I had a father and he asked me to do something for him—I'd do it. I wouldn't let anything in the world stop me."

The boy looked up at her, his face angry. "Listen," he said, "I'm not going to run away, see? Now, shut up about it."

Behind her back Penny was wringing her hands so hard the knuckles were hurting. As she stood looking down at the boy and trying to think of another argument there was a loud thump on the deck just above her head and then another thump. The boy sat up straight, listening, and Penny looked swiftly at Nick.

"They've come after us!" Penny whispered. "Where can we hide?"

A voice from on deck called, "Ben. Oh, Ben."

"Quick! Where can we hide?" Penny demanded.

"Under here," the boy said, sliding back a little door under one of the beds.

Nick and Penny scrambled into the dark little place, and the boy slid the door shut on them again. Then it was pitch dark. Penny slowly straightened out her legs and then felt Nick moving beside her. There was a lot of rope under them, and when they moved the rope made a faint sound. "Ssssh," Penny whispered, her lips against Nick's ear.

32

They heard the boy say, "Good morning, Uncle Pete," and a man's voice said, "Morning, Ben. This is Mr. Sylvester."

Ben said, "Good morning," and another voice said, "How do you do, Ben."

The voices in the cabin were easy to hear where Nick and Penny were. The one the boy had called Uncle Pete said, "Mr. Sylvester is interested in the boat, Ben."

There was a long silent pause, and then Ben said, "How do you mean, interested?"

"Well—er—he wants to buy it, Ben," Uncle Pete said. He sounded a little nervous, Penny thought.

"She's not for sale," Ben said. His voice sounded angry, and Penny could imagine how he looked.

"Now, Ben," Uncle Pete said, "you've got to realize a few things. This is an expensive boat to keep up. I mean, it's expensive for you. You've only got the money your father left you, and it's just enough to take care of you— put you through school and things like that. It isn't enough to keep up an expensive boat like this. You've got to sell it, Ben, and Mr. Sylvester is making a very handsome offer for it."

There was another long pause, then Ben said quietly, "This is my father's boat. He doesn't want to sell her."

"Ben," Uncle Pete said, "I know how you feel and all that, but you've got to be practical. You've got to stop thinking he's still alive. The Navy doesn't think so."

"Because the Navy can't find him doesn't mean he's dead," Ben said.

THE LION'S PAW

Then the tone in Uncle Pete's voice changed. It got angry and hard-sounding and, even though Penny couldn't see what the man looked like, she began to hate him.

"Well, I'm sorry to tell you this, Ben," Uncle Pete said, "but I'm your father's executor until you're twenty-one. If you don't believe that, you can go see the lawyer, but it's true. I can legally sell this boat any time I want to, and I'm going to sell it now. Do you understand? Of course the money goes to you."

"All right," Ben said, his voice so low Penny and Nick could barely hear it.

Penny felt Nick move, and she stopped him with her hand. But all the hope had gone out of her when Ben said, "All right." She thought of the courtyard back at the orphanage. All through the summer she and Nick would spend the play hours walking around and around the graveled yard. They would have to stay ten feet apart and they couldn't even talk to each other. And she thought of her room. Maybe, she thought, she could get them to give her a different room, a room which faced away from the ocean, so she wouldn't have to look at it any more.

Uncle Pete said, "Good boy. I knew you'd be reasonable about it. Now, tomorrow I want you to meet me and Mr. Sylvester at the bank. Ten o'clock. Be on time, will you, Ben?"

"Ten o'clock," Ben said.

Then the voices faded out and Penny and Nick could hear footsteps going away. After a while it was silent.

"Are we going to have to go back?" Nick asked, his voice almost choked with crying.

Penny moved in the cramped little place until she could put her hand on his head. "It won't be so bad, Nick," she said. "Maybe, after a while, somebody nice will adopt us."

"No, they won't," Nick said. "And you know it."

Suddenly the sliding door opened and the boy said, "All right, come on out."

Penny and Nick crawled out on the cabin floor and slid the door shut again. As they got to their feet the boy went over and sat down in front of the maps. He picked up the dividers again and began to twist them between his fingers.

"Could you hear what he said?" the boy asked slowly.

Penny nodded.

"He's going to sell the boat," the boy said. "He's going to sell my father's boat."

Penny nodded again.

The boy lifted one of the maps and reached under it, pulling out a slip of paper. "Tide's high at ten-thirty." He looked up at Penny. "We're sailing tonight," he said quietly.

Tears welled up in Penny's eyes until she had to blink them away in order to see anything but a mist. "Running away?" she asked, her voice husky.

THE LION'S PAW

The boy nodded. "He can't sell my father's boat. I don't care what sort of legal junk he's got. What would my father think when he comes back to find I've let the boat be sold? He wouldn't think I was any good, would he? He'd think that I—didn't believe in him," the boy said.

Penny nodded.

The boy stood up. "Well, I do," he said quietly. "I believe he's coming back."

"I do too," Penny said.

He looked at her. "You do?"

"Yes," she said.

The boy suddenly smiled, then he laughed out loud. Then he made the shrill whistling noise again and said in a loud voice, "Turn to! Sweepers, man your brooms! Clean sweep-down, fore and aft!" He grabbed Nick by both arms and lifted him up off the floor. "Turn to, m'boy," he said; "we've got a lot to do before we sail." He set Nick down again.

"Penny," he said, pointing his finger at her, "you and Nick go forward. Go up that way as far as you can and you'll come to a big pile of chain. That's for the anchor. Get it all straightened out and coiled up so it'll run free. I'm going down to the bank and draw out all my money and then get some provisions aboard this craft. If you get through with the chain before I get back get all the rope out of where you were hiding and coil it all up shipshape."

36

Penny was so full of excitement she couldn't talk, so she kept nodding her head vigorously.

"You better not go on deck," the boy said. "Somebody might see you. The three of us have got to sail this boat for a long time and go a long way."

Penny nodded again, and the boy went bounding up the narrow ladder to the deck. For a moment Penny and Nick stood still, listening as the boy began to sing in a loud voice:

> "For breakfast I eat marlin spikes,
> For lunch a bowl of OAK—um."

Then, when his song had faded away, they looked at each other.

It was hot and stuffy in the cabin because Ben had sealed it up so that no light would show out to anyone who might be on the wharf. The heat made Penny feel how tired she was after all the work they had done that day. She and Nick had coiled up what seemed miles of heavy anchor chain and then more miles of stiff new rope. Then, just as they got ready to sit down and rest, a truck came out on the wharf, and they had to lift down and stow all the provisions Ben had bought. There were sacks of flour and potatoes and meal, dozens of cans of peas and soup and corn and meat. Then there were heavy boxes of tools, bolts, nails, fittings for the boat, more and more rope, more sails, a brand-new anchor. And when that truckload was emptied into the boat and Penny's arms ached from lifting stuff down through the hatches, another truck came with cans of oil and two drums of gasoline, cans of paint, heavy packages of putty, oakum, varnish, and a shiny new brass propeller.

All that day they had made the boat shipshape. The drums of gasoline were securely lashed on deck and, below, everything was stowed away. Once, while Penny was climbing over a mountain of provisions stacked in the main cabin, she had wondered where they were going to sleep and how the boat was going to carry it all, but Ben knew just where to put everything, and now it looked as though nothing had been brought aboard the boat.

Penny looked at the hands on the brass clock screwed to the bulkhead. She had been wondering about the clock all day, for it didn't strike the way other clocks did. At eight o'clock it struck all right except that the strikes came: "Tingting-tingting-tingting-tingting." But at four o'clock in the afternoon it had struck the same number of times.

Now it was almost nine o'clock, and Ben was finishing the letter. Penny watched him write slowly, often pausing to look off vaguely at nothing.

Then he finished. "How does this sound?" he said.

He read:

"DEAR AUNT MARY AND UNCLE PETE:

"I have decided to take the boat away because I don't think it ought to be sold. I don't think Dad would like

38

it, and he would maybe think that I let it be sold because I didn't believe what he said in the letter. He said he would come back and he will, and the boat ought not to be sold.

"Don't worry about me at all. There are two people going with me and both of them are very good sailors, so I will be all right and won't get into any trouble.

"Please don't look for me because I am going to a place where nobody can find me.

"I will write to you often and I will come back when my father does. I love both of you very much. Give little Mary a hug and a kiss and tell her I will send her a present.

"Yours truly,
"BEN."

"That's fine," Penny said. "Except we aren't 'very good sailors.' We don't know anything about sailing."

"That's all right," Ben said. "By the time they get the letter you'll be good sailors." He licked the envelope and got a stamp. "I'll go mail it and be right back."

He turned off the cabin light and went up the dark stairs. After he had gone Penny closed the cabin door and turned on the light again. She looked at the clock, and it began to strike, but instead of striking nine times, it struck only "tingting" and stopped.

"That clock is busted," Nick said.

"I don't know whether it is or not," she said.

"It is," Nick declared. "It runs so slow. Ben said we would sail at ten o'clock, but that old clock will stop

39

going before then." Nick went over to one of the beds which were built into the side of the cabin and stretched out. "Oh, boy," he said, "feel this bed. Just like swimming."

Penny looked longingly at the other bed in the cabin and almost went over to it, but then she thought that it wouldn't look good for Ben to find her lying down after she had said she would work hard and not sleep at all until they had sailed far away, so she sat up straight at the table in the middle of the cabin and looked at the clock. It was five minutes past nine.

"I like Ben," Nick said. "Even better than I liked Sam back at the eganahpro."

"I do too," Penny said.

Nick yawned, and the sound of it behind her made her so sleepy it almost hurt.

"I wish we had a father like Ben has," Nick said, his voice drowsy. "Even if the Navy couldn't find him. It would be somebody to love. All I've got to love is you, but I've been doing that so long I know all about it."

Penny only nodded her head and looked at the clock again. It was six minutes past nine. "It's taking him a long time," she said.

Nick didn't answer, and Penny turned slowly around in her chair and looked at him. He was sound asleep, the light full on his face. As she looked at him, his lips parted slowly and his hand, hanging over the side of the bunk, relaxed. It was the first time Penny had really seen

40

him asleep since she had been moved out of the Baby House six years ago.

"His face is beautiful," Penny thought. Asleep, all the wistfulness was gone. It didn't have that look of almost sad hoping that all the orphans' faces had when they were awake. Nick's face was serene and happy, and he looked much younger than nine.

A wave of love for him swept her and, coming quickly after it, a wave of almost fear. If they were caught and taken back to the orphanage now it would hurt Nick so much. Much more than it would hurt her. Somehow he had never got used to the orphanage. For as long as she could remember Nick had wanted to get away from it; even when he was only five or six years old he had talked about running away. And now, after just this little time of freedom, Nick would never again be able to live at the orphanage with any happiness.

"He's sort of like the ocean," Penny thought, her brain tired and loose with sleepiness. "He wants to be free. Or maybe like a bird flying so far up you could hardly see it."

Penny slowly put her hands, palms together, below her chin and began to pray:

"Our Father Who art in heaven," she prayed, "maybe You think we're doing wrong to run away. Maybe You think we ought to be punished by getting caught and sent back. But, God, Nick doesn't want to go back; he doesn't like it—he hates it—so there must be something wrong with it. Please, God, let us get away in this sailboat. Please don't let anything stop us." She stopped for a moment, then went on:

"But if You think we ought to go back and are going to let us get caught, please let us sail for just a little while. Maybe only for tonight or even some tomorrow when the sun will be shining. It'll give us something to think about when we go back and have to walk the courtyard. We'll think about it all the rest of our lives.

"And, God, even if You let us get caught, please let Ben get away. And, please, let his father be alive. Amen."

Behind her Nick breathed slowly and quietly. Penny glanced up at the clock, then jerked her eyes back to it again. It was twenty minutes to ten. Ben had been gone for more than half an hour.

Terrible thoughts rushed into Penny's mind. "Maybe he's been caught already," she thought. "Maybe he fell off the wharf and drowned." And then slowly she thought, "Maybe he's deserted us. Maybe, because it's dark, he's gotten scared and changed his mind."

Penny turned out the light, then opened the door and ran up on deck. The wharves were as she remembered them from the night before. The wood seemed pale and clean and empty in the starlight. Out in the bay green and red lights flashed, glowed, went out. On a road far away a car's lights moved like a fast firefly.

There was no sign of Ben or of anyone else. Beyond the wharf the lights of the town glowed and a rumbling noise came from it, with notes of music, the steady drone

42

of cars, the noises of people, all mixed together. But on the wharves it was silent, dark, and deserted.

Penny felt the same frantic feeling as she pulled herself up from the boat to the wharf and began to walk down it.

Then she saw the figure running toward her and recognized Ben's white sailor pants and the dark blue shirt. Penny smiled a little to herself and was ashamed of herself for thinking that Ben had got scared and backed out.

He was running fast, his tennis shoes making a hissing noise on the planks. When he got to the boat he said to her in a hoarse whisper, "Cast off! Cast off! They're coming. . . . Untie the boat!" Then he ran past her, jumped down to the deck of the boat, and disappeared into the cabin.

For a moment Penny stood confused, wondering what he meant by "Cast off," then her mind began to function. She ran to the front of the boat where she had seen a big rope tying it to the wharf. She unwrapped the rope, threw it down on the deck, and ran down to the other end of the boat where there was another rope.

As she threw this one down on the deck a sputtering roar came from under the stern of the boat and clouds of stuff like steam came up. Penny backed away along the wharf, but the roar subsided to a steady throbbing noise and she saw Ben run up the ladder to the cockpit.

"Get aboard!" he whispered loudly to her. "Get on!"

Penny jumped down, fell, and crawled back to the cockpit.

43

Ben shoved something with his hand, the roar of the boat's engine got louder, and Penny suddenly saw that the boat was slipping away from the wharf.

"There they come," Ben said in a quiet voice.

Two bright lights appeared on the wharf and swept down toward them, and soon she could hear the motor of a car. The lights swung out on their wharf just as the bow of the boat slid away from it.

Above the sound of the boat's engine they heard voices yelling, "Ben! Ben!" And in the light of the headlights Penny saw Ben clamp his jaws tight as he shoved the tiller over and the boat swung away from the wharf, the long mast raking across the stars.

"Who is it?" Penny asked, whispering.

"Uncle Pete," Ben said.

Then the car horn began tooting. It kept on blowing and blowing and blowing as the boat swung around until the bow was pointing out toward the open sea.

"Let 'em blow," Ben said quietly.

The tooting stopped abruptly; the lights of the car backed away, then swung down the wharf.

"Now Uncle Pete's sore," Ben said. "When people don't do what he says he gets sore. And when he does he's just like a bulldog. . . . I guess we're in for it, Penny."

"In for what?" Penny asked. "Being chased by that old uncle of yours? You know, Nick and I are being chased by a whole orphanage—and we don't care."

"Neither do I," Ben said.

"How'd he find out?" Penny asked.

"I went into Neel's to get you and Nick some clothes and ran smack into Uncle Pete and that Sylvester fellow. They said they were coming down to look over the boat. . . . I bet I broke the world's record for running."

"It was close," Penny said.

Ben said slowly, "This is going to be a battle, Penny."

"I guess so," she said.

"Well, bring 'em on," Ben said. Then he took a deep breath. "I don't care. You know, I feel sort of free already."

"So do I," Penny said.

Chapter 4

THE boat was moving now into the
darkness of the sea. Penny looked back at the town and
saw the band of darkness moving steadily in between the
wharves and the boat. Then she looked ahead toward the
faraway lights of the channel buoys and the Christmas-
tree lights on the two peninsulas which formed the bay.

"Is Nick all right?" Ben asked.

"I'm afraid he fell asleep, waiting," Penny said apolo-
getically. "You know he's only nine years old."

"Let him sleep," Ben said. "This is going to be a long,
long night, and we'll need him—wide awake—before
morning."

"What do you think your uncle will do?" Penny asked.

Ben didn't answer for a moment, then he said quietly,
"He isn't dumb, Penny."

Penny looked slowly around at the dark water and up

46

at the dark sky lit only by the stars. The boat seemed to be so much smaller than it had been when it was moored to the wharf. It seemed to be just a white sliver in all the darkness, with its tall, bare mast sliding along, and behind it a gray thinning trail of water stirred by the propeller.

If Ben's uncle caught them, Penny thought, that would be the end of it for her and for Nick. The boat was like a trap, she thought; it was a cage out on the dark water.

The binnacle for the compass had a dim yellow light flooding the floating compass card, and the light came up and lit Ben's face. Penny looked at him and he looked different. He looked older and more serious as he kept glancing down at the compass, then out again into the darkness. She began to feel better; she began to feel that Ben had strength enough and knew enough about boats to get away from everybody.

"I don't think you're dumb either," Penny said.

Ben glanced at her and smiled. "Maybe not," he said. Then, with his free hand, he patted the deck of the boat. "Not for sale," he said.

"What can your uncle do?" Penny asked.

"I'm trying to figure it out now," Ben said slowly. "I know he'll tell the Coast Guard. And he'll probably ask the Navy to look for us. He might even hire a boat himself."

"Do you think you can sail better than the Coast Guard?" Penny asked.

"No," Ben said. "They've got the cutter and all sorts of surfboats and speedboats. They could catch us—easy—if they sighted us."

"How can you hide, then?" Penny asked. "I don't see how you can hide a great big thing like a boat."

"We can't hide it," Ben said, "but maybe we can put it where they wouldn't think it could possibly be. That's what I'm worrying about now. . . . You see that red light and those other lights under it? That's the Coast Guard station, and we've got to pass it to get out of the bay. If Uncle Pete has already called them up we should try to sneak past without them seeing us. But if he hasn't told them yet we ought to go in close so they can't help seeing us."

"Why?" Penny asked. "If they see us they'll catch us."

"Not unless there's a reason," Ben said. "And if we can put them on the wrong track from the start, we'll have a much better chance of getting away. Blast! I wish I knew what Uncle Pete's done."

"Well, if you wanted to find a sailboat what would you do?" Penny asked.

"*I'd* call the Coast Guard," Ben said. "But Uncle Pete's a funny guy. He hates to think he's wrong. He hates to admit anything. I think that for a little while at least he won't believe that I'm going out of the bay. For a little while I don't think he'll admit that somebody did something he told them not to do. Then, when he does admit it, he'll yell for the Coast Guard, the Navy, the

Merchant Marine, and everything else. . . . And maybe that hour or so he spends fuming around is going to be just what we need, Penny. If we can make the Coast Guard think we went north, while actually we go south, we might get away." Ben pushed the tiller over, and the bow of the boat swung in toward the lights of the Coast Guard station.

"I'm going to sail her right through their dining room," Ben said, a note of grimness in his voice. "And if I'm wrong about Uncle Pete and he's already warned them, all they've got to do is throw a grapnel aboard to catch us."

Penny looked at a channel buoy as it slid past them, its light rocking gently back and forth. "I hope you're right," she said in a small voice.

Ben looked at her. "What will they do to you and Nick if they catch you?" he asked.

"Take us back and punish us," Penny said slowly. "They don't like for the orphans to run away. And afterward they'd watch us—all the time."

"Take the tiller," Ben said. "Just hold it right where it is."

"I don't know how," Penny said.

"It's easy. Just don't move it. I'll be right back," Ben said.

Penny slowly put her hand out and touched the smooth wood of the tiller. As Ben took his hand off she slid hers up until she could feel where his hand had made it warm.

49

She held it as tightly as she could even though she felt shaky, and her throat began to get dry.

Ben went forward and unlashed the little dinghy and swung it over the side. It dropped into the water with a splash, and Penny thought he had thrown it away as it slid past the stern, but Ben came back with the painter and secured it. The dinghy bobbed and slid along in the wake. To Penny it looked as though the little boat were scampering along, trying its best to catch up with the big boat.

"Within ten minutes," Ben said, sitting down and taking the tiller, "we'll find out whether I'm right or wrong about Uncle Pete. If I'm wrong, they'll catch me. But not you. Go below and wake up Nick."

Penny felt so afraid that she stumbled a little as she went down to the main cabin. In the darkness she shook Nick and he sat up, pushing her away with his hands. "Go away! Go away!" he said.

"Nick, it's me," Penny said, catching his hands. "Come on."

"What's the matter?" Nick asked, his voice frightened. "What's the *matter*?"

"Nothing. We're running away," Penny said.

Nick followed her back up to the cockpit and sat down close beside her as he looked slowly around at the dark water and scattered lights.

"You and Nick get into the dinghy when I slow down," Ben said. "The oars are tied under the seats with the oarlocks on them. If the Coast Guard comes after me, I'll cut you adrift and you can get away, and they won't catch anything but me."

Penny looked back at the tiny boat bobbing in the wake. "In that little boat?" she said.

"It's a good boat," Ben said. "If they catch me, just row toward the lights. Land isn't very far, and you can make it all right. When you get to the beach, fill the boat with sand and sink it, then wade along the beach until you're a good way from the boat. Then walk backward across the sand until you get to where your tracks won't show any more."

Ben slowed the engine until the boat was barely making headway and pulled the dinghy in under the stern. "Get aboard," he said quietly.

Penny looked across the dark water at the lights of houses on shore. They looked far, far away, and the water was dark, the reflections of stars swaying back and forth on it.

Penny slowly climbed down into the dinghy and waited for Nick to follow her. Ben patted Nick on the shoulder and said, "If they catch me, good luck to you, Nick."

Nick just nodded his head and came on down into the dinghy.

"Sit down low in the boat," Ben said, "and don't move around. Are you ready?"

Penny and Nick sat down on the floor boards and

gripped the gunwales of the dinghy with all their might.

"I guess so," Penny said.

When Ben started the engine it sent a spray of hot salt water over them. Then the big boat, white as a swan in the darkness, moved away from them. Penny watched it, and it went on and on, leaving the dinghy drifting on the dark water. Just as she began to think that Ben had already cut the rope the dinghy heeled far over, jerked around, and started racing after the sailboat.

It went terribly fast, white water boiling along down both sides, the bow way up in the air and white water gurgling around the stern and almost coming in on them. Spray kept splashing over them in flying sheets until they had to duck their heads and could no longer see anything.

Time seemed endless as they crouched blindly in the bottom of the dinghy. Penny thought, "This is like one of those bad dreams when you keep waiting and waiting for something terrible to happen and all the time you're trying to wake up and can't."

Nick began to shiver with cold, for he was in front of her and most of the water was hitting him. She heard him spit and then say, "Penny. Penny. I'm scared, Penny."

"So am I," Penny said. "But I think we're all right. We must be almost through."

"I'm sitting in the water, Penny," Nick said.

"So am I," Penny said.

"It's awful wet, isn't it?"

"And cold."

"Why did we get in this little boat?" Nick asked.

"We're going past the Coast Guard, and if they catch us they won't catch anybody but Ben. You and I'll sneak away in this boat."

"Oh," Nick said. Then a big splash of spray hit him and she heard him spit again. "Salty," he said.

Penny made her eyes into slits and slowly raised her head. Through the mist of spray hitting her in the face she could make out some low buildings with lights in them and a high steel tower with red lights going up it, but that was all she could see because her eyes began to burn with the salt water, so she lowered her head again.

Nick was shivering hard, and his voice shivered also when he said, "Running away is certainly hard work, isn't it?"

"Yes," Penny said. "Harder than I thought."

"It's worth it, though," Nick said. "I'd rather be here even if I am sitting in a lot of water."

"So would I," Penny said.

The boat went on and on. Penny looked up again and could see the big boat up ahead with Ben sitting alone in the cockpit. He was looking forward, and the Coast Guard station was falling away behind them. Penny tried to listen for the sound of another boat, but she couldn't hear anything above the noise the water was making around the dinghy and the panting of the engine as the exhaust pipe dipped in and out of the water.

Suddenly their boat stopped. The bow dropped and the whole boat settled down in the water until they thought it was sinking. Then it began to move slowly forward again and was soon up under the stern of the big boat with Ben leaning down toward them.

"You all right?" he asked.

"Yes," Penny said.

"All except I'm drowned," Nick said.

"Climb up," Ben said. He helped Nick up and then Penny, and as they stood on deck shivering and wet he hauled up the dinghy and dumped the water out of it before putting it back on top of the cabin house and lashing it down.

"Let's get going," Ben said, coming back to the cockpit. "I haven't seen any sign of them chasing us, but there's no use taking any chances. You and Nick go below and change your clothes."

"Into what?" Nick asked. "I've got on all the clothes I've got."

"That's right," Ben said. "Get some of mine out of the chest in my cabin. Don't let the light show."

Penny was shivering so hard she could hardly talk, but before she went below she asked, "Do you think we got away, Ben?"

"So far," Ben said. "I know the man in the tower saw us go by and head north because I could see him myself. We'll find out whether it fools 'em."

Penny looked at Ben's face lit by the binnacle light

BEFORE PENNY WENT BELOW SHE ASKED, "DO
YOU THINK WE GOT AWAY, BEN?"

and felt better. She thought, "With Ben helping us, we'll get away all right." She liked Ben; she liked the quiet way he went about doing things.

Down in Ben's little cabin across from the galley she and Nick shut all the ports and turned on the light. Nick's hair was matted on his head, and his lips were almost blue with cold. She helped him off with his clothes and found a big bath towel for him to rub with, then she got some more clothes out of Ben's chest and Nick put them on. They were much too big for him, even with the pants and sleeves rolled up. The shirt hung in folds from his shoulders, and the pants almost went twice around his waist. He tried on a pair of Ben's tennis shoes, but they were so big he couldn't even keep them on his feet.

"Then I can go barefooted?" Nick said.

"Until your shoes dry," Penny told him.

"Sailors don't wear shoes," Nick said. "In the pictures they're always barefooted, with their pants rolled up."

"We'll ask Ben," Penny decided. She got some more pants and a shirt and put them on. They were too big for her also, but she didn't look as floppy as Nick. But Ben's tennis shoes did not fit her either. Penny looked up from where she was sitting on the floor. "Maybe I can go barefooted too," she said.

"We'll ask Ben," Nick said.

They went back up to the cockpit where Ben was sitting with one of the maps spread under the binnacle light. He had the dividers again and was measuring along the map. Penny watched over his shoulder as he made a little ring and wrote "Departed 2309 16 June. Speed 6, course 005." Then he looked up and saw Nick.

"Feel better?" he asked Nick.

"A lot," Nick said. "Ben, don't sailors go barefooted?"

"Most of the time," Ben said.

"See?" Nick said to Penny.

"Do you go barefooted, Ben?" Penny asked.

Ben pulled one of his tennis shoes off with his toes and then the other one. "I always went barefooted when Dad was aboard. Uncle Pete wouldn't let me, though."

"They never would let us go barefooted," Penny said. "Nick threw his shoes away one time and he had to work in the kitchen for a month."

"Can I throw my shoes away, Ben?" Nick asked.

"Keep 'em," Ben said. "You'll need 'em where we're going."

"Where are we going?" Penny asked.

"To find a Lion's Paw," Ben said quietly. He unfolded the map, spreading it over his and Penny's knees. "Here's where we are," he said, pointing with the dividers. "We left the last channel buoy at nine minutes past eleven. We'll keep going north for two hours—that'll put us past the next Coast Guard station. Just as soon as we get out of sight of that we'll turn and go due east. Then south, then west. By dawn tomorrow I want to be right here." He pointed to a little curve of the coast line. "There's a

58

place we can hide the boat there, and tomorrow night we can start out again."

"Where are the Lions' Paws?" Nick asked.

"Way over here," Ben said, pointing to the other side of the map.

"How far is that?" Penny asked.

"I don't know. A long way," he said.

Penny looked up from the map and was surprised at how dark it was everywhere. There were no lights, no flashing buoys, no land. "Is this the sea, Ben?" she asked, almost whispering.

"Yep," Ben said. "This is the Atlantic Ocean."

"I've looked at it a lot," Penny said. "But it didn't look so big."

Ben chuckled and folded up the map. "As oceans go, this is a pretty fair-sized one," he said.

"How deep is it?" Nick asked.

"Not very, right here," Ben said. "Five fathoms."

"What's a fathom?"

"Six feet. But in some places it's more than two thousand fathoms."

"Is it dark down there? Even in the daytime?" Nick asked.

"Yep," Ben said. "My father said that it was so dark way down that the fishes that live down there have their own lights so they can see where they're going and what they're looking for."

"Is this a good boat?" Nick asked. "It won't sink or anything?"

Ben laughed. "Don't worry, Nick, it isn't going to sink."

"I didn't think so," Nick said. "But I just wanted to know."

"Why don't both of you go get some sleep?" Ben asked. "I'll wake you up when there's something to do."

The thought of the bunk down in the main cabin almost made Penny fall asleep where she was, but she didn't want Ben to think that she and Nick were just passengers on his boat.

"No, we'll stay up and help you," she said.

"There's nothing for you to do. And tomorrow there will be. Go on below, both of you."

"All right," Nick said. "Good night, Ben."

"Night."

Nick stopped at the head of the companionway. "They would have caught us by now if it hadn't been for you, Ben," he said.

"They may yet," Ben said.

"Well—maybe so," Nick said. "But even if they do, we've been away more than a whole day already."

Penny followed Nick to the companionway. "If you need us, wake us up, Ben."

"I will. There's a buzzer down there that I can ring from right here. If you hear it, come on topside."

"All right. We won't sleep very long. Just a little," Penny said.

"Sleep until I ring the buzzer," Ben said. "Good night."

Down in the cabin, Penny and Nick looked at the two bunks, one on each side. "Which one do you want?" Nick asked.

"It doesn't make any difference. You take the one you were in."

They were both in bed with the light out within a minute. Around them they could hear the noises of the boat; the steady slow throb of the engine, the wash and slide of water against the hull, the little creaking noises a boat makes under way. The open hatch made a rectangle of stars and sky.

Penny slowly relaxed. When she thought of the huge empty darkness of the sea she felt a little afraid, a little as though everything they were doing was too big for them to do and they would have to stop. But when she stopped thinking about it she felt sleepy and peaceful and happy.

Hours later something woke Penny up, and she lay for a minute listening, trying to find out what it was. Slowly she realized that the engine wasn't throbbing any more.

Penny got out of bed and went to the companion ladder. Ben was still sitting at the tiller, his head and shoulders framed against the starlit sky.

"Ben," Penny called in a loud whisper. "Ben."

"What?"

"What's the matter?"

"Nothing," he said. "Six bells and all's well."

"What's the matter with the engine?"

THE LION'S PAW

"We're under sail," Ben said. "Go to sleep."

Penny went a few steps up the ladder until she could see out. Above her the white sail was like a smooth cloud with the starlight on it seeming to make it almost glow. She stood for a moment looking up at it and, without any reason, she felt like crying. She wasn't at all afraid. Instead she felt happier than she ever had before. It was just the curve of the sail and the whiteness of it.

She went back to her bunk and lay for a while, listening. The water went faster past the boat now, and it didn't seem to splash against it the way it had when the engine was running. The boat just seemed to be swimming along in the water, with the wind making it go and the sea not minding the passage of the boat across its darkness.

Chapter 5

ENNY was dreaming that she was standing outside the tall iron gates at the orphanage. The children, inside the gates, were walking slowly along the graveled paths. They were all dressed in white clothes and they weren't playing. There wasn't any laughter, and none of the little ones were chasing one another. They were just walking slowly around and around, and they wouldn't come to the gate and listen to her. Penny wanted to tell them something and she kept calling to them by their names, but they wouldn't even turn their heads toward the gates. So at last Penny decided to go in to them and tell them. She put her hand on the long iron handle of the gate and turned it, and the gate began to swing open, but as it did something behind her made a terrible buzzing noise which got louder and louder as she swung the gate open.

THE LION'S PAW

Penny sat up straight in the bunk and stared around. It was pitch dark, and the buzzing noise kept on and on. Penny lay back down again and jerked the covers up to her chin, but the buzzing went on and suddenly she remembered Ben telling her about the buzzer.

Penny jumped out of bed and ran to the companionway. "We're coming," she called up to Ben, and then went over and shook Nick until he woke up.

In the cockpit Ben was studying the chart carefully when Penny and Nick joined him.

"I think we're at the right place, but it's so dark I'm not too sure. I've never been in here at night."

Penny looked up, away from the dim binnacle light, and slowly she could see the deeper darkness of land resting on the darkness of the sea.

"We haven't got much time," Ben said, "so we'll have to take a chance. Penny, you go forward—go up as far as you can and let me know everything you see. Nick, you go up halfway and repeat everything she says. But don't make any more noise than you have to because we don't want to wake up the fishermen who live along the banks."

Ben put the chart where Penny could see it too. "It'll be dawn in less than an hour," he said. "You see where this river comes in, Penny? We're going straight up the river until we get past the third big bend. Past that there's a little inlet where we can hide the boat. Now remember how this looks. Keep us in the middle of the river until

64

after the first bend, then keep us way over to the left-hand bank around the next one—there's a sand bar sticking out from that. Then over to the other bank. Watch out for floating logs and for fish nets. You can tell them by the rows of stakes sticking up out of the water. If you see something, tell Nick what it looks like; whether it's to the left or the right of the boat, and which way to turn. Say 'Turn left a little' or 'Turn left hard,' or if you can't tell which way to go, say 'Stop.' "

"All right," Penny said.

"Nick, you repeat everything she says just exactly the way she says it, hear? And if you tell me something and I don't say 'O.K.,' then run back here and tell me again. Just be sure that I hear what Penny says."

"All right," Nick said.

"Boy," Ben said, "I hope this is the right river."

Penny hoped so, too, as she went along the deck until she could go no farther. There was a steel rope going up from the bow of the boat to the mast, and she got outside of that and wrapped her leg around it so she wouldn't fall off.

Then she looked forward. She couldn't see a thing but pitch-black darkness.

Penny was panic-stricken as she stared into the black wall. How could she even tell where the river was? she wondered. Maybe there was something right in front of the boat that they would run into within the next second.

65

But as she kept looking the darkness seemed to form itself into shapes and shades of blackness. Straight ahead there didn't seem to be anything except water, but on each side, far away, the real deep darkness seemed to go up a little higher than it did in front.

Behind her the boat was silent, the light wind in the sails noiseless as it blew gently against Penny's face, and she could hear only the little lip-lapping of the water against the bow. Without turning around she said, "It looks like land on each side of us, but we haven't reached it yet."

Then she heard Nick say, "Penny says it looks like land on each side of us, but I can't see it at all."

"Nick," Penny said, whispering sternly, "you say what I say and nothing else."

"Well, I don't see anything," Nick whispered back.

"That doesn't make any difference," Penny said. "*I* can see it."

"I bet you can't," Nick said.

"Oh, Nick!" Penny said in exasperation. "You'll never be a sailor if you don't do what the captain of the boat says."

"All right," Nick said. "Say something."

"Wait until I see something," Penny said.

After a while she said, "The darkness looks closer on the right-hand side."

"Penny says the darkness looks closer on the right-hand side," Nick said.

66

"That's better," Penny said.

"That's perfect," Nick said.

The boat swung slowly to the left. Nick said, "Ben wants to know how that looks."

"It looks even now," Penny said.

The boat stopped swinging and kept on going into the darkness, the night wind dying in the sails as it blew from the shore. Ghosting along, the boat was like a white cloud as it went gliding into the mouth of the little river.

"We must be in the river," Penny whispered, "because there aren't any more waves."

Now the boat was absolutely silent, the lip-lapping of water at the bow gone, the creaking of timbers hushed as the strain of the open sea and the wind was taken away.

Penny saw a lighter shade of darkness sticking out, and after a while she whispered back to Nick, "There's a long thing like a wharf over to the left." She listened as Nick whispered it back to Ben.

Then Nick said, "Ben says this is the right river. Keep going straight ahead."

They slid past the rickety fish pier, and in the darkness Penny could just make out the shapes of some wooden sheds and shacks and in the water some long, low rowboats. On the right bank a rooster crowed, and across the river a dog woke up and barked sleepily and went to sleep again.

The river narrowed above the little settlement, the dark banks crowding in toward the boat. Penny stood in the bow, straining her eyes and whispering directions back to Nick and Ben. As the false dawn came with its graying darkness Penny was able to make out the shapes of trees and dark shadows on the water she learned were stumps and logs. With the wind dying before the rising sun, the boat slowed until it hardly seemed to make its way against the current of the river, but at last Ben whispered, "This is the place." And the sound of the sails coming down seemed very loud to Penny, although it was only the whisper of folding canvas, linen rope in sheaves, the faint metallic clicking of the guides in the runners.

The anchor made a white, spreading splash in the black water, and Ben appeared beside Penny. Pointing, with his arm close to her cheek, he said, "We want to tow her stern first up that little creek, Penny. I'll go ashore with a line. Get Nick to stand in the stern, and as soon as he feels me jerk three times on the line, you get the anchor up; just lay it on deck. Then, as she goes in, fend her off the banks with the boat hooks."

Penny nodded, and as Ben went aft she went to look for the anchor chain. Nick came up soon. "You know what he did?" Nick said. "He dove right off into that black water."

"What?" Penny asked in amazement.

"Yes, he did," Nick said. "He took a big coil of rope and just dove right off. You see that splashing? That's Ben. Do you think an alligator will eat him?"

"Oh no!" Penny said, straining her eyes to watch Ben

68

swimming toward the dark bank. At last she saw him—a spot of gray moving in the darkness. "Run back and hold the rope, Nick," she said. "Whisper when he jerks it."

Nick went running aft, and Penny got the anchor chain in both hands. Soon Nick's loud whisper came and she began to haul up the wet smooth chain. In a little while she could feel slimy mud on it, and then the ring bolt of the anchor. It took all her strength to lift it over the gunwale and put it down, black with mud, on the clean deck. Then she went aft to where Nick was standing.

"Where're the boat hooks?" she asked.

"The what?" Nick asked.

"Didn't Ben show you the boat hooks? He said to fend off with the boat hooks."

"He didn't tell me," Nick said. "He just said don't let it hit the bank or get the mast tangled up in the trees."

Penny, on hands and knees, started feeling around for the boat hooks and at last found two of them lashed together beside the cockpit. By the time she got them unlashed and gave Nick one the boat was moving slowly stern first toward the dark bank of the river. Penny and Nick stood on the quarter, holding the boat hooks down and out from the boat. Whenever the shafts struck anything they would both push away from it.

Slowly, as Ben made his way along the bank, sometimes splashing along in the shallow water, sometimes wading knee-deep in the oozing mud of the bank, they warped the boat far up the narrowing creek. As it moved,

69

the trees, clothed in dripping rags of Spanish moss, seemed to crowd in closer and closer. They towered above the straight slim mast, and before Ben finally stopped hauling, the spreaders were catching in the moss and tearing it loose.

There was a faint and delicate arch of pink in the sky when Ben finally made his line fast to a tree on shore and climbed back aboard the boat. Birds in the forest around them began to stir and chirp, and a mockingbird suddenly burst into clear, loud song, so close that it sounded as though it were on board with them. The noise of the woods grew and grew as the sun came up and showed the gray thin mist clinging to the surface of the river.

Ben was covered with black, dripping mud all the way up to his eyes. In the light of dawn Penny and Nick stared at him, and when the mud broke around his mouth and he laughed, they did too.

Ben got a collapsible canvas bucket tied to a short length of rope and dipped it over the stern. Penny poured it over his head and Nick scrubbed him with the deck swab. Slowly they got the mud off him, and when he was dry enough they all went below.

"I'll cook while you get dry," Penny said.

"Fine. Do you like music with your cooking?" Ben asked as he turned on a radio in the main cabin.

As music filled the boat and the smell of bacon began to come out of the galley, the sun rose high enough so that light flooded down through the skylights and drove

SLOWLY THEY WARPED THE BOAT FAR UP THE
NARROWING CREEK.

away all the night's darkness and chill. Nick finished setting the table in the main cabin and came back to sit on the flour bin, watching Penny.

"This is wonderful," Nick said slowly. "I knew all the time it was going to be like this."

Ben was whistling in his little cabin, the bacon was frying, and the coffee was beginning to boil on the back of the Shipmate. The radio played something about a beautiful morning, and when it got to the part about an elephant's eye Nick sang as loud as he could, "*EYE*," and began to drum on a shelf with a long spoon.

Ben came out in a little while in a clean pair of faded khaki pants. "I still feel like I've got mud on me," he said.

"Did you see any alligators?" Nick asked.

"Not many. Just little ones," Ben said, and winked at Penny.

"I want to see one," Nick said. "Could you get a little one so I could keep it in a bottle?"

"Sure," Ben said. "You can take it to bed with you if you want to."

"Breakfast is ready," Penny said. "You men go sit down."

Nick looked at her, then stood up and marched into the main cabin. "Have a seat," he said to Ben, and sat down at the head of the table.

Ben walked slowly around to Nick's chair and picked it up, Nick and all, and put it down at the side of the

73

table. "What sort of navy is this?" Ben asked. "The boot seaman sitting in the skipper's place? Looks like mutiny to me."

"Is this a navy?" Nick asked. "A real one?"

"Yes, it is," Ben said. "It may not be the biggest navy in the world, but it's going to be the best."

"Am I in it, Ben?" Nick asked.

"Yes, sir. You're the rank and file."

Nick looked very pleased. "What are you?"

"I'm the captain."

"Is Penny in it too?"

"She's the quartermaster."

"I'm the cook," Penny said, bringing in the breakfast. "But the rank and file does the dishwashing."

"Is that right, Ben?" Nick asked, his voice sad.

"Nope," Ben said. "All hands share the ship's work in this navy—including the captain."

As Penny ate she glanced at Ben sitting at the head of the table. His eyes were tired and there were little veins in them, and in a little while he rested his head in the palm of one hand while he ate with the other.

"We'll keep quiet, Ben," Penny said, "and you can sleep all day."

"I believe I could sleep for a week," Ben said. "But I think we'd better all sleep as much as we can today because tonight is going to be harder than it was last night."

"I'm not sleepy," Nick said. "I'll go and catch an alligator, maybe, while you sleep."

THE LION'S PAW

Ben smiled sleepily at Nick. "That mud would just swallow you without even gulping," he said.

By the time they finished breakfast the radio was reciting the news. None of them listened as they carried their dishes back to the galley, but when the announcer said, "And now we turn to the news of local interest. Runaway children seem to be heading the list this morning," Ben stopped in mid-stride, then slowly put his plate down and went back into the cabin. Penny and Nick followed him slowly, and all three of them stood motionless in front of the loud-speaker.

"Mr. Pete Lanford," the announcer went on, "has requested that all fishermen, yachtsmen, and people along the coast keep a lookout for his nephew, Benjamin R. Sturges, who, Mr. Lanford reports, has apparently run away. Young Sturges, a boy of fifteen, is sailing a thirty-foot white sloop-rigged yacht named the *Hard A Lee* and is believed to have aboard two of the children from the local orphanage—Penelope Brown and her brother Nicholas—aged twelve and nine years old."

Penny and Nick gasped simultaneously.

"Young Sturges," the announcer continued, "is the son of Lieutenant Ben Sturges of the Navy, who was, before his death in action, a well-known and -liked yachtsman in Florida and Caribbean waters. Mr. Lanford reports that he knows of no reason why the boy should run away from his pleasant home and thinks that it is merely a boyish prank. However, afraid that young

75

Sturges may be overreaching himself, he has asked the Coast Guard, the Navy, and all merchant ships to report the position of the yacht if it is sighted and to try to take it in tow.

"The yacht is believed to have left the bay last night as the Coast Guard at two places has reported a yacht of that description sailing north.

"Nothing is known of the background of the two orphans, but they are believed to be aboard the yacht, as various trades-people who delivered provisions to the boat yesterday afternoon report two children aboard who answer the description of the escaped orphans.

"Mr. Lanford is posting a sizable reward for information regarding the whereabouts of his nephew. I repeat—Benjamin R. Sturges, a fifteen-year-old boy, has gone to sea with a twelve-year-old girl and a nine-year-old boy, both from the orphanage, in a white, thirty-foot sloop. It was last seen sailing north in open water. Please notify this station if you have seen or heard of this boat.

"And now for Florida and south Georgia weather forecasts. . . . Clear today . . ."

Ben clicked off the radio and turned slowly to look at Penny and Nick.

Chapter 6

S PENNY stood in the suddenly silent cabin she could feel the trap closing in on them again, the freedom they had known slipping away. Already the talk and laughter at breakfast, the memory of the white sails spread in the darkness, the waking from the dream to find herself far from the iron gates seemed long ago. The trap was closing, the space of freedom they had narrowing, the doors slamming shut on them. The Coast Guard, the Navy, the Merchant Marine, all the thousands of people who listened to radios were hunting them. They could never escape all that.

Ben walked slowly over to the table and sat down. There were some crumbs from the toast in front of him, and he licked his forefinger and picked them up one by one and ate them. Nick went over and sat down on his

77

unmade bunk, and Penny walked over and leaned against the open door. The sun was well up now; outside the boat bugs and birds were talking back and forth to each other; a squirrel was barking at something which had entered his little kingdom. Looking up the companionway, Penny could see a roof of trees above the boat, the Spanish moss a grayish silver in the sunlight.

All the crumbs were gone from the table, and Ben began pulling gently at the lobe of his left ear.

Nick finally broke the silence. "Maybe an alligator will eat your uncle, Ben."

"They wouldn't want him," Ben said.

Then he looked at Penny. "There's one good thing," he said slowly. "They think we went north."

Penny nodded. "He said that twice."

"I'm not much worried about the Navy—they're too busy to bother with one little sloop. But the Coast Guard isn't. And these fishermen see everything that goes on. They're the ones who'll turn us in."

"Where do they live?" Penny asked.

"All along the coast and around the lakes," Ben said. "You saw their houses when we came up the river last night."

Penny nodded.

"One of them is liable to come poking in here any time," Ben said.

"Do they have radios?" Nick asked.

Ben nodded. "A lot of them do."

78

"Suppose we went out in the woods and lived like Indians?" Nick said.

Ben shook his head. "Even the Indians can't live in the woods any more, Nick. There isn't enough game, enough food."

Ben got up and went to the door where Penny was standing. "I wish I could get it straight in my mind," he said quietly. "We've got to get moving; we've got to get to Captiva—but it's a long way."

"What's Captiva?" Penny asked.

"A little island," Ben said. "There are Lions' Paws there. If we could get there, they'd never find us."

"How far away is it?" Penny asked.

"It's over off the other coast, in the Gulf of Mexico."

Ben went over to a little bookshelf, got a key, and slowly wound the clock. Soon after he finished, it struck four bells.

Suddenly Ben turned to Penny. "He said 'a white sloop named *Hard A Lee*,' didn't he?" Ben asked.

Penny nodded.

"Well, this is going to be a black sloop named *Lion's Paw*," Ben said quietly. He went over to a drawer and got some money. He gave Penny and Nick each some of it.

"Here's what we're going to do," Ben said. "There are two little fishing villages near here—one north about five miles and the other down at the mouth of the river. I can't go to either one of them because Dad and I used to come here a lot to fish, and the people might recognize

79

me, so you two will have to go. Penny, you go north—I'll row you across the river and show you the road—and, Nick, you go down-river. Get as much black enamel paint as you can carry and bring it back. By nightfall there won't be any white sloop named *Hard A Lee*."

Penny felt excited, and slowly the doors of the trap seemed to stop closing. They didn't open any wider, but they stopped closing.

Then Ben looked at her. "You've got to be a boy," he said. "Nick, get the scissors out of that drawer."

Penny raised her hands to her faint gold, long hair done in two braids around her head, then she slowly lowered them.

"Come up on deck where the hair won't get all in the boat," Ben said.

It didn't take very long. When he finished Ben stood back, looking critically at it, and said, "A little ragged, but most of the kids around here are too. And you'll have to stay barefooted, Penny. Shoes would be a dead giveaway."

Penny's head felt light and a little cold. She watched as Ben swept the waving masses of golden hair ruthlessly across the deck and sluiced them off the boat. Then he got the dinghy into the water, and Penny climbed down into it with him.

On the other side of the river Ben pulled the dinghy up out of sight and led Penny along a deer trail through the forest. As they went away from the river the ground got dry and hard and began to hurt her tender feet, but she didn't say anything to Ben about it. When they came at last to a narrow, deeply rutted dirt road Ben pointed down it. "It's about five miles, Penny. On your way back look for this arrow." He drew an arrow in the dirt pointing toward the woods. "I'll draw some more along the trail as I go back. When you get back to the river, whistle and I'll come get you."

"All right," Penny said. She turned and started down the road.

Then Ben joined her again. "If anyone asks you what you want the paint for, tell them to paint a coffin," he said. "That's about the only thing I know to paint black."

"All right," Penny said. "Good-by."

" 'By, Penny." He looked at her for a moment, then smiled. "Don't worry," he said quietly, "we're going to get away."

"I know it," Penny said, and walked on down the road. She looked back once, but Ben had disappeared into the forest. Penny clutched the money in her pocket and walked on, picking her way and trying to step only on the soft, sandy spots. Ben's pants felt funny flopping around her legs, and there was hair down inside the collar of her borrowed shirt.

Sunlight sifted down through the leaves which crowned the road, and the huge trees crowded close to each side of it. All sorts of little tracks and lanes and furrows marked the gray dirt, and on each side of her there was a continuous rustling of little wild things invisible in the woods.

Penny felt very lonely as she walked. In her whole life

81

she had never gone anywhere by herself. At the orphanage there was always someone with you from the time you got up until you went to bed. You even marched to meals and classes and work periods. There was always someone to talk to or, if you didn't want to talk, you knew that when you did someone would be there to listen.

Penny began to whistle. She whistled "Onward, Christian Soldiers" for a while and then the song that Ben liked to sing: "A Marlin Spike Bosun." But she kept feeling lonely, and the road was so long and so empty, and in the forest all the bugs had another bug to talk to and all the birds talked all the time.

Whistling didn't do much good, Penny decided after a while. She stopped in the road and stood on one foot for a minute and then on the other one because both of them were getting sore. While she was standing there two little squirrels began chasing each other up and down a tree. Penny was surprised at the way they could run straight down the tree, their feet hardly seeming to touch it, without falling off, and when they got almost to the ground they could turn around and run straight up again.

When Penny started walking again she noticed a blue-and-white bird sitting on a low limb beside the road. The bird was yelling its head off, making a loud raucous noise in the woods, but when she got closer to it, it stopped yelling and just sat there looking at her. Without thinking what she was doing Penny said out loud, "Good morning, bird."

THE LION'S PAW

The bird didn't say anything, but when Penny walked on past it the bird began to yell again. She looked back at it and said, "Good-by, bird."

The sound of her voice made her feel less lonely and she said, "This is a long old road." Then she said, "My feet hurt."

She half expected someone to answer.

She said, "Benjamin R. Sturges. Ben Sturges. Ben and Penny and Nick put out to sea in a pea-green boat. No, a black enamel boat named the *Lion's Paw*. . . . They're running away, and everybody is hunting for them. Everybody wants to catch them." Then she said slowly, "But nobody wants them. Old Mrs. Wertz just wanted Nick to do all her work for her; she didn't want to love him or anything like that. And old Uncle Pete doesn't love Ben—at least not the way Ben's father does. . . . I wonder what's going to happen to us. I wonder if anybody is ever going to love us. If Ben's father comes back he'll love Ben, but what about me and Nick? Is anybody ever going to love us? Everybody has somebody else to love, so they haven't got any room for me and Nick."

Penny felt very sad until she thought, "If Ben's father is really dead, the way the Navy says he is, then he won't come back. And if he doesn't come back, then we can all love each other. We'd get along fine."

That made her feel better and she walked a little faster.

At each bend of the road Penny expected to see the town when she got around the corner, but every time there was nothing but more road, another bend. Her feet were getting very painful, and the left one had a cut on the side of the big toe where she had stepped on a sharp rock buried in some sand. For a while the cut had bled, leaving a little pink spot at each step, but now it wasn't bleeding any more and was caked with blood and dirt. But both her feet were burning, and each time she stepped down the ground felt like the top of a stove, and even soft roots felt as hard as stones. She kept twisting her legs so she could see the bottom of her feet and she always expected one of them to be raw, but they didn't look much different, just dirtier.

The dog barking was the first sign she had of people living near the road. The dog ran out at her and barked, then kept following behind her and barking. Once she turned around toward it, and the dog sat down in the sand but didn't stop barking. Finally it gave up, and Penny walked on toward the houses she could see up ahead. They were all as gray and old-looking as the Spanish moss; none of them had any paint, and they looked as though they were about to fall down.

Then Penny reached the oyster-shell road. She took two steps on the crushed shell and stopped because the stuff felt like broken glass to her feet. Down the road she could see a few weather-beaten automobiles, some faded store signs, and some people moving around. She took another step, and the oyster shells hurt so, she had to swallow to keep from crying. Walking on tiptoe, she went to the side of the road where some grass was, but she had walked only a little way before she got into sandspurs and had to go back on the shells again.

Penny stopped and looked at the stores. Then she said to herself, "If you're going to cry, you'd better cry now and get it over with because they'll suspect something if you cry when you get to the store." Then she waited to see if she was going to cry, but she didn't.

At last she got to the stores where there was a sidewalk made out of wood in front of them. The wood felt almost soft after the oyster shells. One store had a faded sign reading: "Hardware. Supplies. Boats Built," and she walked into it.

A man in the back of the store was putting things on a shelf, and when Penny opened the door a cowbell clanged and the man looked at her. "What you want, young'un?" he asked.

"Some paint, please," Penny said.

"House paint or boat paint?"

Penny thought for a moment. If she said boat paint he might get suspicious, "Just black enamel paint," she said.

"Black enamel!" the man said. "What you gonna paint with that?"

"A coffin," Penny said.

The man looked sad. "Oh, too bad, too bad," he said. "How much you want, son?"

"As much as I can carry," Penny said.

"How fur you totin'?" the man asked.

Penny stopped to think again. "Ten miles," she said.

"You're a little puny," the man said. "You'll do good to tote a gallon. You got any money?"

"Yes, sir."

"Lemme see some."

Penny held out the money Ben had given her. The man nodded and got a gallon can of paint. It looked small to Penny, and she was sure she could carry more than that. "I want some more," she said.

"Now, hold up," the man said. "This is more'n enough for a coffin."

Penny swallowed. "Well," she said, "there are a lot of coffins. There's a coffin for—er—Buddy and—er—Pa and Uncle Pete and Mrs. Wertz. Lots of coffins."

"Oh, too bad, too bad," the man said. "House burn or fever?"

"House," Penny said.

"Who's left alive?" the man asked, getting another gallon.

"Well, Maw and—er—Junior," Penny said.

"Sad thing, sad thing," the man said, reaching for the money. Penny gave it all to him and he counted it slowly, licking his thumb for each bill. "Hardly enough," he said, "but—under the sad circumstances I'll just let it be enough."

"Thank you very much," Penny said.

"Not at all, son. Glad I could help you in your bereavement."

86

THE LION'S PAW

Penny picked up the two cans of paint and almost put them down again. They were heavy as lead, and she thought of the long, long road. Then she suddenly thought of Ben sitting at the tiller all night long while she and Nick had slept. With the cans of paint bumping against her legs she went out of the store.

Penny didn't cry until she had gone around two bends of the dirt road. Then she put the paint down, sat on one of the cans, and wept. She shifted her feet to a soft, dusty spot, but even there they throbbed and throbbed. Her hands were numb from the thin wire handles of the paint cans, and her shoulders ached from the weight of them. Leaning over with her head on her crossed arms, her tears fell down into the dust and made little round, dusty balls which gradually disappeared.

At last Penny blew her nose violently on her shirttail and stopped crying. Leaving the paint in the middle of the road, she went over to where she could reach some Spanish moss and pulled some of it off a tree. She wrapped this around the handles and started off again.

She was resting when the dog appeared. It came up from behind her in silence, crossed the road, and sat down. Penny didn't think it looked angry, and as she watched it just sit and look at her she decided that it looked sad. Its eyes were sad and its mouth and ears were drooping.

"Bow wow," Penny said, not very loudly.

The dog thumped its tail in the dust but didn't come any closer.

THE LION'S PAW

Deciding that it was too sad to bite her, Penny picked up the paint and started walking again. The dog got up and walked, too, but she noticed that it was very careful to stay all the way across the road from her. The dog gave Penny a little comfort, for it looked as sad as she felt, and she was so absorbed in the dog and her feet and hands and back that she didn't hear the wagon until it was almost on top of her. Two old mules were pulling the wagon and a lanky man was sitting on the plank seat.

"If you want a lift, git on behind," the man said. "But I can't stop for you because if'n I do these mules will lay down right where they stop and I'll have to build a fire under them to get them up again."

Penny had to trot a little while she got the paint in the back of the wagon, but at last she pulled herself in and sat for a moment, fighting back more tears until her feet stopped hurting.

"Come on up to the seat where it's a sight more uncomfortable but better company," the man said.

Penny limped up the wagon and sat down beside the man.

"What's your name, son?" the man asked.

Penny said the first boy's name she thought of, "Sam Wilder."

"Wilder? Old Josh Wilder's grandson, I take it, or great-grandson."

Penny nodded. "Is that your dog?" she asked, so he wouldn't talk any more about old Josh Wilder.

88

"WHAT'S YOUR NAME, SON?" THE MAN ASKED.

"I hate to admit it," the man said, "but that old fool dog belongs to me. Or *he* thinks he does."

"Don't you like him?" Penny asked.

"Off and on," the man said. He reached into his hip pocket and pulled out a slab of black tobacco. "Chaw?" he asked, holding it out toward Penny.

"No, thank you," Penny said.

"A smoker, eh?" the man said. "Ruin your health, smokin'." He reached back into the wagon, got a piece of dry mud off the floor, and threw it at the dog. The dog stopped running along beside the wagon and dropped behind.

"Went huntin' with that old dog last night," the man said, biting off some of the tobacco and putting the rest back in his pocket. "Was after coons, but that old dog decided he knew better than me what was a coon and what was a skunk. He declared it was a coon, and when it went down a gopher hole that old dog went right down behind it. I seen the smoke of that skunk rollin' up outa that gopher hole and I said to myself, 'That'll teach that old dog the difference all right.' An' when I pulled that old dog out by the tail his eyes was rollin' around in his head like two marbles and he couldn't hardly stand on his feet. An' I said to that old dog, 'Now, you just stay away from human folkses until that stink you got dies off somewhat.' An' he's so ashamed of hisself that he won't come near a person. How far you goin', son?"

"Almost to the river," Penny said.

"What you got in them cans? Lard for your mama?"

Penny didn't say anything.

"Glad to see folkses able to git lard agin," the man said. "I got to a time there when I was cookin' pancakes out of corn meal and engine oil. Got sorta used to it after quite a spell."

Penny kept watching for the arrow Ben had made on the side of the road. The man kept talking, stopping only long enough to spit over the wagon wheel, and the mules kept moving along, their heads bobbing up and down between their skinny shoulders.

Penny saw the arrow but she didn't say anything. She waited until the wagon had gone around a bend before she said, "I'll just hop off the back. Thank you for the ride."

"Glad to do it. Give old Josh my re-gards."

"I will," Penny said. She took the paint and got down into the road without stopping the mules. The dog trotted wide around her, and the wagon disappeared around the next bend in the road.

Penny turned and went back toward the arrow. The ride had done her feet a lot of good, and she soon reached the riverbank where she whistled and watched for the dinghy.

Ben had black paint splashed on his arms and two or three places on his face. "We've almost finished a quarter of it," he said. "Gosh, you got two gallons! Fine. Nick could only get a gallon."

92

"I got a ride in a wagon," Penny said.

"You made a quick trip, Penny. Are you tired?"

Penny was so tired she was afraid she wouldn't be able to stand up again, but she said, "No. I'm all right." She looked at the muscles working in Ben's bare back as he rowed, and she thought, "I wish I had some muscles like that. I wish I really was a boy."

Chapter 7

BEN had closed the cabin tightly so the lights wouldn't show and it was hot, but it felt good after the cool of the river's evening mist. Penny was sitting on the edge of her bunk, her pants legs rolled up, her feet in a bucket of brine. She lifted up one dripping foot and looked at it. It was pink and swollen a little.

"Do you think this stuff will get them tough enough to walk on tomorrow, Ben?" she asked.

"There won't be much walking to do," Ben said. "It'll take all night for the paint to dry, so we'll have to stay here all day tomorrow."

"What will we do?" Nick asked. "Work?"

Ben shook his head. "Just lie around and wait for dark."

"Then since there's nothing to do at all, I don't see why I couldn't go hunting for an alligator," Nick said.

"You can. But while you're hunting for a little one be sure a big one isn't hunting for you."

Nick looked less brave. "Don't they make any noise?"

"Not in the water, and when they get up where you are they just slide along in the mud."

"Well," Nick said, "I'd better wait until somebody can go with me. They can look behind and I can look in front."

"I'll go with you when my feet get tough," Penny said. She leaned back in the bunk until her shoulders touched the wall. Tiredness seemed to come down on her like the water from a hot shower bath. It flowed all down her muscles, and her eyes just wouldn't stay open. She would open them as wide as she could and look all around the little cabin, but soon they would close, no matter what she did.

"A girl at the orphanage had a doll," Penny said sleepily, "and when you tilted it, its eyes would shut. After a while"—she yawned so wide her jaw cracked—"after a while the doll got broken and we could look inside of its head and take the eyes out. The eyes were the bluest things you ever saw. But in back they had a wire, and on the end of the wire was a piece of lead, and that's what made them open and shut." She yawned again and wiggled her toes in the brine. "That's what I've got on my eyes, lead weights," she said. "When I lean back my eyes just have to shut."

Ben, sitting at the table, stretched and yawned also.

95

Then he scratched his head furiously and stood up. "Me for the sack," he said. "Good night."

"You aren't going to bed?" Nick asked. "Who'll I talk to?"

"Penny," Ben said. "Good night."

"She doesn't know anything about alligators or anything," Nick said.

Ben looked at Nick. "Nick, my boy, you're just a young man. But me, I'm an old man and I needs me sleep. I'll talk to you about 'gators tomorrow."

"All right," Nick said, his voice resigned.

"Good night, Ben," Penny said. Then she turned on Nick. "Don't you ever get sleepy or tired or anything?"

"Not me," Nick said. "I'd go 'gator hunting right now if I knew where to go."

"Go to bed!" Penny said. She lifted her feet out of the bucket and let them drip, then she wiped them with her shirttail. "After you turn out the light open the—hatch," Penny said.

"Hatch? Oh, door," Nick said as he switched off the light.

From her bunk Penny heard Nick slowly going to bed. After he was in it he said, "This is a real navy, isn't it? Hatch and everything."

"Well, that's what Ben calls it," Penny said.

"We've got to learn all the words," Nick said. "Like 'sack.' He means his bed when he says that."

"And starboard and port."

96

THE LION'S PAW

Penny was almost asleep when Nick said, "I think the boat looks better all black this way. It looks more piraty."

"Mm," Penny managed to say before she went to sleep.

In the morning the black paint was dry and the new name, for which Ben had cut a stencil so it was neat and professional-looking, gleamed white at the stern and on the two life-preserver rings lashed to the stays: *Lion's Paw*.

Nick was the first one up. For a while he played around the boat, trying not to make any noise, but he would forget and his bare feet would sound like horses walking around on the deck, so at last Penny and Ben got up also.

After breakfast they wiped all the varnished wood with soft cloths and fresh water, swabbed the deck, flemished down all the lines, and put what Ben called a Sunday furl in the sails. By the time they finished the sun was coming down hot through the green roof of leaves and limbs above the mast. The three of them sat in the cockpit and scrubbed all the galley gear until even the iron frying pan gleamed.

Penny's feet were much better, but she soaked them in brine again after lunch while Ben gave them both a lesson in boat handling, the nautical names for things, and knot tying. After that he took Nick out in the dinghy and taught him how to row while Penny sat with her feet soaking and watched Nick try to make the little boat go straight up and down the creek the way Ben did.

97

THE LION'S PAW

When they came back Ben lashed the boat down on the cabin skylights. "We'll sail when the tide turns about eleven tonight," he announced. "That'll put us into Stuart around three in the morning if the wind holds. So by dawn we'll be in the St. Lucie and on the way."

"What's the St. Lucie?" Nick asked.

"It's a canal. I'll show you."

Ben brought up the maps, which they had learned to call charts, and he showed them the way they had to go. At a little town on Florida's Atlantic coast they would enter the St. Lucie Canal, which would lead them to the huge Lake Okeechobee. They would cross this lake and enter the Caloosahatchee Canal and then the Caloosahatchee River to Fort Myers and the Gulf of Mexico.

Ben stopped his moving finger there. "And then," he said, "we start looking for the Lion's Paw."

Nick looked up from the chart. "I'm glad we're going so far away from the eganahpro, but, Ben, what good is a Lion's Paw, anyhow? A lady gave me a sea shell one time and I kept it for a while—remember, Penny?—but then I threw it away because it wasn't good for anything."

"I used to think that too," Ben said quietly. "Then my father began sending his shells to me, and he used to write about them. Wait a minute."

Ben went down into the cabin and came up with the steel box in which he kept all his father's letters. He got out a letter and settled down cross-legged in the sun.

He read:

THE LION'S PAW

"DEAR SKIPPER:

"I'm sending you another batch of shells today and hope that FPO gets them to you. They should just about drive Pete and Mary out of the house by the time they get there because I haven't had time to clean them and the people living with me aboard ship have declared that I can't clean any more shells in the cabin. And I can't much blame them.

"I got the face mask you gave me for my birthday, and the boxful of stinkers is the result. I can't tell you where I found them, but I had a good time doing it. Whenever I get off the ship and into the face mask everything seems to change. The ship is so hot, so crowded, so noisy. If it isn't the bugle, it's the gongs, and if not the gongs, then it's an airplane engine or dozens of airplane engines, and if the airplane engines are all right, it's the twenty-millimeters, the fifty-calibers, the forties, the five-inch—and sometimes it's the whole works—guns, motors, bugles, gongs, bells, buzzers, catapult. You know my sack is about one foot below the catapult sheave. I have to climb up and slide under the thing, and if I should hump up my stern while they're catapulting I would immediately become a much thinner man. They catapult the planes with an acceleration from zero to about ninety miles an hour in a hundred feet, so by the time the catapult goes down my bunk it's doing ninety and making a fearful racket. They usually catapult just after I've gone to sleep after standing a midwatch.

"The Navy is a very noisy place, as I said. There isn't a minute of the day or night when something or somebody isn't making a loud, official noise. But under the sea it is silent—or almost. The faint crackling noise I only hear at

99

first. It's like eggs frying with the galley door shut. I wonder what makes that noise. Is it the chewing of all the millions of things in the ocean? They must eat all the time.

"I hope these shells are reaching you, Skipper. I often wonder when I go ashore and find old FPO in some muddy tent—at one place the post office was just where the officer in charge of it happened to be—or, after we've been on an island a while, there's a big quonset hut with Fleet Post Office in nice letters—where was I? Oh, yes, I often wonder if these little boxes I put down, and a sailor with nothing on but khaki shorts picks up, ever reach you. They have so far to go, these little boxes full of cotton and fragile shells. I don't even live in the same day with you now because we are well on toward Japan. I don't even live in the same hemisphere half the time. Sometimes I start to think about how many miles it is, but after I get past five thousand I stop thinking about it—five thousand just about reaches the Pacific coast.

"When I get back we'll do some cataloguing—if we can find the names of the shells. We'll take the *Hard A Lee* and sail off about a hundred miles from the coast. Then we'll heave her to and just sit there, undisturbed, and figure out what kind of shells are which and I'll tell you where I got them—from which of the hundreds of islands we've visited, in pursuit of the little yellow man, I found this shell or that one.

"In the meantime you get busy too. I'm sending you a book called *Florida Sea Shells* by a real conchologist named Ethel Snyder who lives with a little dog named Dolly Varden over on Sanibel. I think, before I get back, you'll have time to find them all except the Lion's Paw."

Ben stopped reading. "That's what he thinks about them," he said quietly. "They mean a lot to him—and me too. They're—beautiful," Ben said.

"Have you got any?" Penny asked.

Ben looked at her and smiled. "I've got them all," he said. "Sometimes FPO took months, but they all came— even the last boxful. He sent me that just ten days before he—before he got to be missing."

"Will you show them to us?" Penny asked.

"I want to see a face mash," Nick said.

Ben laughed. "That's a good name for it. After an hour or so you feel like your face has been mashed. But it's a mask. I'll show you."

Ben came up with a big wooden box with a hinged lid, and a shoe box. He put the big box carefully down on the floor of the cockpit and opened it. There was a layer of white cotton, and he lifted that away and laid it aside.

In a shallow wooden tray divided into sections were dozens of sea shells. Penny looked at them, expecting to see the kind of shells she knew about—the white, bleached curved shells or gray wrinkled oyster shells—but in the sunlight the shells in the box were wonderful. They were of all colors and shapes, from deep orange to the faintest tinge of blue and green. There were round, glass-smooth shells, which looked like the eyes of cats made with jewels.

Ben lifted out tray after tray of shells. Some of them were fantastically shaped with long spines; others were as clear as glass and tissue thin. There were tiny little clear blue balls, little dishlike shells with mother-of-pearl gleaming inside; there were conchs, cowries, volutes, olives, tritons, murices, pectines. There was a chambered nautilus with part of the outer shell cut away so that they could see the little silver rooms, one after another. There were hundreds—thousands—of sea shells.

Penny had never seen anything as beautiful, and she sat on her haunches for a long time just looking at them.

Without saying anything Nick held out his cupped hand. Ben picked up one of the cowries—a domed shell with a faint blue tinge and a clear polished gold ring around the top—and dropped it into Nick's hand. Nick sat down, carefully balancing his hand, and stared at the shell. Then with one gentle finger he turned the shell over on its back so that he could see the perfectly formed opening of deep, satiny purple. "Does anything live in there?" he asked, and didn't know that he was whispering.

"Something did," Ben said.

"I bet he hated to die," Nick said, giving the shell back to Ben.

Ben put all the trays back into the box, put the cotton pad on again, and closed the box. Then he opened the other one. There were three rubber face masks with heavy glass fronts. He tried one on Nick, the rubber covering his face in a circle from the top of his forehead down around his eyes and along his upper lip. Nick peered out through the heavy clear glass.

"I can see good," Nick said.

Penny tried on the other one, and she and Nick put their faces close together and looked at each other through the glasses.

"I want to try mine in the water," Nick said.

"Too muddy. Can't see a thing. Wait until we get into the Gulf," Ben told him.

"Will we use these to hunt for Lions' Paws?" Nick asked.

Ben nodded.

"We'll find one," Nick said. "We can see them lying around."

Ben nodded and put the face masks back in the box. "Won't Dad be surprised when he comes back and we've got one?" Ben asked. "We won't show it to him at first; we'll just wait until he says something about not having one, then we'll show it to him."

Penny looked at Ben. "What does he look like?" she asked.

"My father? Well, he's big. He's more than six feet tall and he weighs almost two hundred pounds. But he isn't fat. He's got more muscle than anybody you ever saw. He can pick up the dinghy and hold it straight out with one hand."

"Does he look like you?"

Ben shook his head. "He's sort of good-looking. He's got sort of gray eyes with little wrinkles around them from sailing so much and he's got white teeth. One of the front ones is broken off a little from when I jibbed her all standing and the boom hit him. I was only a little kid then, though, and didn't know much about sailing."

"Are you like us and haven't got any mother?" Nick asked.

"She died when I was born," Ben said.

"Ours didn't die until I was two years old," Nick said.

"Three," Penny said. "I remember."

"You do not," Nick said.

"Yes, I do. She was in a white room with some flowers and she had long black hair."

"Maybe so," Nick said.

"Didn't your father ever get married again?" Penny asked, ignoring Nick.

Ben shook his head. "He almost did one time, but she always got seasick on the boat, so he didn't marry her."

"Didn't he work or anything? Didn't he have a job?" Nick asked. "Did he just sail around all the time?"

"Sure, he worked. He built sailboats. He built this one."

Nick looked around the boat in amazement. "He did? How?"

"He knows how. He built the boat that won the Bermuda race. He's built a lot of boats."

"Hmm," Nick said. "That's funny. I never thought about how a boat got to be a boat. I guess I thought they just grew."

"Did you help him?" Penny asked.

104

"After school and in the summer. But most summers we would just sail around. Dad said we were looking for customers to buy his boats, but we hardly ever went where there were very many people."

"Just you and your father on this boat?" Penny asked.

Ben nodded.

Penny looked at the slanting bands of sunlight coming down through the forest above them. "Ben," she said, her voice low, "what's it like to have a father?"

"How do you mean, Penny?"

"I mean—well, does a father tell you not to do things, and to do things, and to go work, and get up and go to bed? Does he boss you around?"

"Well," Ben said, "he was the captain of the ship."

"Did he—did he love you, Ben?"

Ben looked at her. "Well, I guess so. We didn't talk about it."

"Did you love him?"

Ben stirred restlessly and looked at the top of the dark river. Then he nodded.

"Didn't he ever say, 'Ben, I love you'? Didn't he ever say, 'Ben, my son, you are a fine boy'?" Penny asked.

Ben shook his head. Then he smiled. "Once in a while he'd say, 'Mate, we've got a fine crew aboard this vessel,' and there wouldn't be any crew except me. And sometimes," Ben went on slowly, "he'd put his hand on my head or my shoulder. Not for long. Just put it there and then take it away."

"How did you like that?" Penny asked.

"All right," Ben said.

Penny thought for a while, then she said slowly, "When he comes back do you think he'll mind about— me and Nick?"

"We don't get seasick," Nick said.

"He won't mind. He'll like you," Ben said.

"Are you sure?" Penny asked.

Ben looked at her. "Yes, I'm sure."

"He must be a nice man," Nick said.

"My father is the finest man in the world," Ben said quietly.

Chapter 8

ARKNESS was coming before sun-
set as the sky was slowly being covered by a low overcast.
While Penny and Nick set the table in the cabin for
supper Ben went to the companionway and looked up at
the solid gray of the sky through which the sunlight was
soft and also gray. Going up the ladder a few steps, Ben
tapped with his fingernail on the face of the barometer.
The needle showed no tendency.

"Blast!" Ben said.

"What's the matter?" Penny asked.

"I don't think we're going far tonight," Ben said.
"There isn't going to be a breath of wind, and I'll bet you
five cents it rains. No cloudburst, just a good steady
drizzle."

"Well," Penny said, "this is a good place. Nobody could ever find us hidden in here."

"No, they couldn't," Ben agreed, "but just the same I want to get out of here. I don't like this feeling of having land within spitting distance all around. I want a little sea room. And I want to get out of the Atlantic, Penny. By now Uncle Pete's probably got things really organized to find us on this coast. So I want to get over on the Gulf Coast."

"How long do you think it'll be this way?"

"There'll be wind tomorrow—plenty of it," Ben said. "We'll get out tomorrow night." As he went topside he added more cheerfully, "As long as we're safe here I don't really mind not sitting out in the rain all night."

It was almost dark when the long, narrow boat came snooping into the creek where the *Lion's Paw* lay moored. A lone man in the stern sculled the boat with an oar, and it slid silently toward the black sloop and was alongside it before Ben saw it. Penny and Nick were still down in the galley, and Ben said in a voice loud enough for them to hear him, "Good evening."

"Howdy," the man said.

Nick started out through the cabin, but Penny grabbed him by the seat of the pants.

"I want to see who it is," Nick said in an angry whisper.

"Ssssh," Penny said. "It may be somebody looking for us, you dope."

"Oh," Nick said. Then he climbed up on the drainboard so he could look out through the half-opened sky-light. He whispered down to Penny, "It's a man in a little boat. I never saw him before."

"What's he doing?"

"Talking to Ben."

"What's he look like?"

"He's little and he hasn't shaved and he has a very sharp face."

"Does he look like anybody from the orphanage?"

Nick shook his head.

Then they listened to Ben and the man talking.

"Nice boat you got," the man said. "Belong to you?"

"To my father," Ben said.

"Mind if I git aboard?" the man asked.

"Well . . ."

"Thanks."

Nick said, whispering, "He's climbing up. He's bare-footed."

"Never seen such a nice boat," the man said. "Mind if I look around?"

"Go ahead," Ben said. "But don't go below. We're fumigating below, and the stuff will make you sick."

"Cockroaches?" the man asked.

"Cockroaches," Ben said.

"Terrible to get rid of. Where's your father, bub?"

"He'll be back," Ben said.

"Gone to town?"

"Hunting," Ben said.

"For what?" the man asked. He had a suspicious, whiny voice.

"Just hunting," Ben said.

"That all there is aboard, just you and your daddy?"

"And cockroaches," Ben said.

"You know," the man said, "when I first seen your mast sticking up in them trees—sort of hid away like—I said to myself, 'That's that runaway boat with them kids on it.' I said to myself, 'Beany'—my name's Bean—'you're just about to make yourself the easiest two hundred and fifty dollars you ever will make.' So I sculled up this creek, but this ain't the sloop they're talking about on the radio."

"I heard about that," Ben said. "White sloop named the *Hard A Lee*, wasn't it?"

" 'Twas. And I was mighty disappointed when I come into this creek and find me a black sloop name of—name of——"

"*Lion's Paw*," Ben said.

"But then I seen you and you answer some to the description of that boy who run off with the sloop—only you look older'n fifteen—anyway, I see you and I think to myself, 'Beany, what's the easiest thing to change on a boat?' And I say, 'It ain't a bit easy to change the rig of one; a sloop is a sloop and a yawl is a yawl. Them are things hard to change. And the lines and the length and the beam, you can't hardly change them.' Then I thinks to myself, 'The very plumb easiest thing is the name, and next to that the color.' And then I remember yesterday I heard about this whole fambly being wiped out in a house

110

burning and a little boy coming to town to get two gallons of black enamel paint."

The man stopped talking, and Penny licked her dry teeth with the tip of her tongue.

Then the man went on: "You know, my wife she says I'm the best-hearted man in the state of Florida. She says whenever I hear about something sad happening to folks I go right now and help 'em out. So, soon's I hear about this terrible house burning, I start looking for the bereaved to help 'em out. But nobody around here has heard anything about it and nobody around here ever before saw that little boy what bought the paint.

"So . . ." the man said slowly, "here I am, but you say this is your daddy's boat and he'll be back, and —I—believe—you, son. I don't really think you're the boy that run away with that sloop and those two little orphans. I don't believe you bought that paint and painted this here boat black.

"So . . . I don't git the two-hundred-and-fifty-dollar reward that fellow Pete Lanford is offering for information. I just don't git that money."

"That's too bad," Ben said.

"Ain't it? I'm sore in need of that money. Well, I'll be going along, son."

"Good-by," Ben said.

"So long."

"He's climbing down," Nick whispered.

Then the man's voice was dimmer. "Son," he said,

"when your daddy gets back you might as well tell him he's got to fumigate this boat all over again. Because the skylight is open, and all that gas just escaped harmless into the air. You ain't killed a single one of them cockroaches, boy."

"That's the cabin skylight," Ben said. "We're not fumigating that."

"My mistake," the man said, his voice fading as he began to scull his boat. "It looked to me like that would be where the galley is, what with the smokestack right beside it!" Ben didn't answer, and Nick craned his head so he could see. Suddenly Nick ducked his head. "He's coming back," Nick said.

They heard the man's voice again. "And tell your daddy he might as well stay here in the creek overnight, son, because there ain't going to be a breath of wind tonight, but it's going to rain a-plenty. It'd be a miserable night for going anywhere."

"Thanks," Ben said, "I'll tell him."

"So long," the man said.

Penny and Nick were waiting in the main cabin when Ben came slowly down the ladder. He walked in silence over to the table and sat down. His shoulders slumped, and when he lifted his hand to pull at the lobe of his ear Penny saw that his fingers were trembling a little.

It seemed to Penny that she could still hear the man's whiny voice, and she suddenly remembered once she had stuck a splinter deep into her hand and it had become infected before she had finally gone to the head nurse at the infirmary. The nurse was a little like that man: she had a sharp face, and on her chin and her upper lip there were sparse dark hairs. She wasn't very gentle with the needle and she had probed around in Penny's hand for a long time, sometimes hitting the splinter and hurting worse than ever. That probing was just like that barefooted man's voice—just picking and picking at things.

Ben suddenly spoke. "He knows who we are," he said quietly.

"I think so too," Penny said.

"He'll be back," Ben said.

"Will he get a policeman?" Nick asked.

"He'll get somebody. Uncle Pete, maybe. He could phone and Uncle Pete could drive down here in a few hours."

"We'd better go then," Nick said.

Ben turned and looked out through the open companion hatch. The sun had set and it was dark, the sky completely clouded over.

"We can't, Nick," he said in a low voice. "There's no wind. We can't use the engine because they would hear it and they'd stop us before we got out of the river's mouth. We're just caught in a trap."

Penny remembered the way Ben had hauled the boat up into the creek with the rope. "Couldn't we pull it out?" she asked. "Nick and I could go along the bank and pull on a rope."

"In the river it's too shallow," Ben said. "We d go aground, Penny."

"Get stuck?" Nick asked.

Ben nodded. "This boat is a devil when she goes aground," he said. "There's a deep keel, and it slides into the mud and sticks."

"Maybe we could paddle it," Penny said.

For a second Ben smiled at her, then he shook his head.

"Well, let's get all the food we can carry and start running," Nick said. "We could run a long way and they'd never find us in these thick woods, would they?"

"I thought of that," Ben said. "But—well, I don't want to leave the boat, Nick. This boat is more home to me than anywhere, and it's got all Dad's things in it. We'd have to carry them too."

"I don't either," Penny said. "If we run away from the boat we might as well—just go back to the orphanage."

"We could hide," Nick said. "We could all three get in the dinghy and row over to the other side and hide. Then when they went off to look for us we could row back again and sail away."

Ben looked over at him. Topside a soft sheet of rain went across the deck, and Penny could see it falling straight down through the open hatch.

"The dinghy," Ben said; "I'd forgotten it." Then he stood up. "We'll tow her out with the dinghy," he said. "Penny, you and I'll row and Nick will steer. We'll slip her right past that snooping rascal."

THE LION'S PAW

"Row all the way down the river?" Penny asked.

Ben nodded. "If we can stand it. But—I don't want to get caught just hiding up this little creek, Penny. I don't want to be sort of like a rat in a hole! If they're going to catch us at least let's give 'em a fight. We'll row that dinghy until we can't row it any more. Maybe we'll make the open sea, maybe we'll have to give up right at the fish pier, but anyway we won't be just sitting here waiting for them to come take us."

"All right," Penny said.

Ben smiled slowly. "Someday we'll be sitting around with nothing to do and we'll say, 'Do you remember that night we rowed?'" Then he laughed. "We'll remember it all right."

Ben started for the hatch. "Right now we've got plenty to do. We've got to get everything white off the boat. Sails, rope, life rings—everything that will show white."

The three of them went up the companion ladder into the softly falling, steady rain.

The *Lion's Paw*, her black hull and stripped topside almost invisible in the rain and darkness, swam slowly out of the creek mouth into the broad darkness of the river. Ahead of it the little dinghy crawled, the two oars making pools of swirling gray.

Penny and Ben sat on the amidships thwart of the dinghy and each pulled an oar. Back on the *Lion's Paw*, staring into the rain, Nick steered the sloop, at first in wide curves and sweeps of the tiller, but as the two boats crept along he steadied down and kept the bow of the *Lion's Paw* pointed toward the stern of the dinghy.

Penny had trouble at first, but Ben kept teaching her and after a while she stopped catching crabs, which almost pitched her backward off the thwart, and settled down, pulling almost as hard as Ben, so that he did not have to stop every few strokes to let her swing the bow his way.

For a mile the current of the river helped them a little and it was not too hard, but the current gradually stopped as the incoming rush of the tide pushed up the river. Steadily the weight of the *Lion's Paw* grew greater against the pull of the oars.

The rain was soft and chilling. Penny could see it, close beside the dinghy, falling into the river and making a thin fog of mist about an inch high. In a little while she was soaked to the skin everywhere, and gradually she realized that the rain did not help as she had thought it would. It made the handle of the oar slick and hard to hold and it made the thwart under her hard to sit on.

Within the first mile Penny got tired. At first rowing had been fun after she had learned how. She liked the feeling in her arms and shoulders; she liked the way it got to be easy after she learned not to fight the oar, not to grip it with all her strength, not to jerk it through the water. She had learned to watch the gray splotch of Ben's hands on his oar and to move her own hands back and forth the way his did. She learned to give the little extra

116

tug at the end of the stroke and then to turn her wrists down and bring the feathered oar forward close over the water instead of lifting it high and waving it around.

Then the slippery handle began to hurt her hands; the wet denim of her pants and the slippery thwart began to rub her; the steady pulling began to ache in the muscles of her arms and back and legs.

"How far have we come?" she asked, whispering.

"A mile or so," Ben whispered back. "How do you feel?"

"Fine," Penny said. She looked through the rain back at the sloop. She could make out the mast and stays against the darkness and the black cutwater sliding through the mist of falling rain. She thought of Nick. Nick was sitting back there on a soft cushion with a huge raincoat on and a sou'wester hat whose brim came down over his back and shoulders. All he had to do was push the gentle tiller an inch this way or an inch that way. He wasn't even getting wet.

Then they reached the tide rip. In a curving line from bank to bank of the river the incoming tide meeting the outward flow of the river made a line of gray-white water. In this conflict of currents the water was shoved up into short, vicious, choppy waves which made, above the gentler sound of the falling rain, a faint roaring noise.

The dinghy writhed and plunged, bounced from a wave top and smashed into the narrow trough and staggered up the next one. Both Ben and Penny caught crabs as the little slapping waves ran out from under the pulling

117

oars or rose up on the forward stroke and knocked the oar out of the oarlock.

"Blast!" Ben said in an angry whisper as the *Lion's Paw* lost way and began to be pushed back up the river by the tide. "Let's try ramming it."

For a minute or so they sat idle while the sloop pulled them out of the miniature storm back into the calm of the river. Penny slumped over the indrawn loom of her oar, the rest feeling wonderful.

"Let's get as much speed as we can and see if we can't jam her right through," Ben said. "Ready?"

"Yes," Penny said, sliding her oar outboard again.

The grayness of his hands began to move once more. They went far toward the stern of the boat, and her hands followed his and then they pulled, the oars biting down into the water, swirling backward, flashing out, and biting again.

Penny gritted her teeth and rowed, her breath sizzling out into the rain, her eyes blinded by it. She put all her strength against the oar, again and again and again.

The dinghy crashed through the first line of waves and Ben said, "Pull!" as the towline came up taut and dripping from the water and the sloop bore down on the tide rip.

They were going to get through the little band of vicious waves, Penny thought as she leaned over and pulled back, her bare feet jammed against the ribs of the dinghy, her heels in sloshing water.

118

THE LION'S PAW

It wasn't enough. The towline slacked off, then snapped up out of the water as the *Lion's Paw* hit the rip. The dinghy was hauled backward up the river again.

Penny could hear Ben panting beside her. Then he sucked in the rain water around his mouth and spat viciously into the bilges.

"We'll try along the shore," Ben said. "Maybe it won't be so bad."

With the oar feeling like lead Penny began to row again. They slowly turned the sloop toward the far shore and rowed along beside the roaring tide rip until at last Ben said, "We'd better try her here. I'm afraid to take her any closer."

Penny looked over her shoulder at the white band of water and suddenly thought, "It's just like the walls and the gate at the orphanage. We can't ever get through it. We'll just butt against it until we haven't got any strength left—just like all the eganaps butted against the walls."

She felt as though she had been rowing the boat for hours, for nights which had no days, for a long, long time.

"What if we don't get through?" she wondered. "When the day does come we'll just be here for everybody to see." That sharp-faced little man would see them, and Ben's Uncle Pete. She and Nick would go back behind the walls again.

They hit the tide rip again. Penny could feel Ben's shoulders moving in unison with hers as they dipped and swung the oars. She wondered vaguely if the muscles she could feel ached as much as hers did.

Then they were through. The dinghy slid down the last wave into quiet water again. Penny sighed with relief and Ben said, "Pull!" and she began to row again. Behind them in the rain the mast of the *Lion's Paw* waved wildly against the dark sky as it hit the rip, then she came through also and slid down toward the boat.

"We've got to get her back in the channel," Ben said, still rowing. "There's shallow water ahead. . . . You O.K.?"

"Yes," Penny said. She was so out of breath that the air she sucked in seemed to burn her throat.

Then the *Lion's Paw* went aground. The towrope stopped the dinghy with a wrenching jerk, and Ben said, "*Blast* it!" and stopped rowing.

"What's the matter?" Penny asked.

"She's aground—and there's the fish pier," Ben said, pointing.

Penny wearily turned her head and could see, through the thick veil of rain, the lights of the fishing village at the mouth of the river. The rain made the lights sparkle like wet stars, but they seemed far away to Penny—and of no importance. She was almost glad the boat was aground because she could rest. She pulled her oar in and bent over it, her whole weight slumping, the rain running out of her cropped hair, running down her face, over her closed eyelids, into the corners of her open mouth.

120

THE LION'S PAW

"Tired?" Ben asked, his voice close and low.

"I think so," Penny said.

"I am too. Let's let her sit there. In an hour the tide will float her off anyway, and I don't see any sign of Uncle Pete."

Penny sighed with relief. She knew that she couldn't possibly push the oar out and drag it through the water even one more time.

Ben turned the boat with his oar and headed it back toward the motionless sloop. "I'll put you aboard and then drop an anchor out into the channel, so when she floats she won't go aground again."

"All right," Penny said, but she didn't even think about what he was saying. Her mind felt numb, and all it could think about was the aching in her body, the burning of her hands.

Suddenly Ben stopped rowing. "Listen!" he said, and turned his head toward the fish pier.

Penny heard the rain falling and heard the little roaring of the tide rip. She didn't want to hear anything else, but the soft throbbing of a motor pushed its way through the other sounds.

"There it is," Ben said, whispering.

Penny pulled herself slowly upright and looked toward the far bank. At first she could see nothing but darkness, but as she turned her head at last she saw a green light, low on the water, moving steadily up the river.

"Is—is that Uncle Pete?" Penny asked slowly.

Ben's voice was flat. "I think so. I can't think of any reason for a motorboat to be going up the river in this sort of weather and at this time of night. . . . Penny?"

"What?"

"Can you row any more?"

Penny curled her stiff fingers around the handle of the oar and slowly pushed it out toward the water. "Yes," she said.

"As soon as they find us gone they'll be back. We've got to get her moving again, Penny."

"Yes," Penny said.

Ben suddenly patted her wet shoulder, his hand making a soft, wet, splashing sound. "I said we'd remember this night," he said quietly. "But if we can get her afloat again we've got a chance. If we don't—they'll find us, stuck in the mud."

Penny began to row again.

She was so tired; her body hurt so badly; her hands felt as though she were holding them in flames. There was no room in her mind to think about what Ben was doing; she just rowed when he rowed, stopped when he stopped.

Ben dropped a kedge anchor far out astern of the sloop. Going back, he and Penny climbed aboard, where Nick was waiting, and a new torture started for Penny's hands as they began to haul in on the anchor rope. Ben would take the rope in both hands, brace his feet against the gallows frame, and haul in until his body came down

almost flat on the deck. Then Penny and Nick, also hauling, would slip the rope around a bitt, brace their feet,
and hold fast while Ben got a new grip and hauled again.

Inch by inch, with the rain pattering steadily down,
they simply dragged the *Lion's Paw* backward, stern first,
out of the mud. The thick, new, wet, rough, hard rope
was more painful to Penny's hands even than the handles
of the oars, and her tears fell down with the rain.

Then the sloop floated again. Penny slumped down on
the deck and sat there while Ben went on working, getting in the anchor, turning the sloop back into the
channel. Then he came over to her.

"One more mile, Penny," he said. "How about it?"

Penny heard him. "I can't do it," she thought. "I can't
get down in that little boat and row any more. I think my
hands are bleeding now." She held them palm up, close
to her face, and tried to see if there was blood on them,
but it was too dark.

"I just can't row any more," she thought. "I can't bend
my fingers so they'll hold onto the handle of the oar."

But she stood up slowly and walked back without saying anything and followed Ben as he got down into the
dinghy.

As Ben slid his oar out toward the water, on which the
rain made a crisp frying noise, he said, "I'm about shot;
how about you?"

"I'm tired," Penny said.

Ben dipped his oar. Automatically Penny began to follow the movements of his gray hands—back and forth, back and forth.

In a few minutes Penny began to cry again. The water running into her mouth got a faintly salty taste from her tears, and the crying made it hard for her to breathe. She clamped her lips shut so Ben wouldn't hear her and went on crying as she leaned forward and pulled back, leaned and pulled.

Now the lights of the fishing village were abeam, the string of wet lights going out on the fish pier moving toward them. Slowly, slowly, they were fading back into the dark rain.

"Half a mile," Ben said.

"All right," Penny said.

After a while Ben said, "I think we've made it, Penny."

"What?" Penny said vaguely.

Ben put one of his hands down on top of hers. "Let me have it," he said. "You move up."

"No," she said, and pushed his hand away.

They rowed in silence for a long, long time. "You're all right," Ben said finally.

It made her feel good. It made the pain feel less. She leaned forward, dipped the oar, swung back, putting all her strength in it.

"I think we've got about an hour's start on him," Ben said. "Fifteen miles." He put his hand on hers and stopped the movement of her oar. Through the rain the sloop glided slowly toward them until its bows were rubbing against the dinghy. Ben climbed aboard it and reached down with both hands. Catching her wrists, he lifted her out of the dinghy.

"Go below," he said, "and fix your hands, Penny."

"All right," she said.

In the dark cabin she felt her way along. Then when her fingers touched the soft dry edge of her bed she stopped. For a moment she stood perfectly still, then, suddenly crying again, she stripped off her wet clothes, dropped them in a pile, and got into the bed. For a long time she shivered violently, but at last the warmth of the covers began to seep into her. Drowsily she heard the throbbing of the engine, the surge and glide of the sloop as it entered the open ocean.

In the cockpit Ben and Nick sat huddled against the rain. When a faint breath of wind stirred Ben raised his head, feeling the wet wind on his cheeks, turning his head slowly from side to side to find the true direction.

"Go below and see how Penny is," Ben said.

Nick got up and sloshed down into the cabin. He came back in a moment. "She's asleep," he said.

"Good. Her hands must be in terrible shape," Ben said. "I've been rowing all spring, and even mine have blisters."

"We went so slow," Nick said. "Was it hard?"

"Yes," Ben said.

The wind breathed again, whirling the straight-falling rain around the yellow light from the binnacle.

"Nick, old boy," Ben said, "we're on our way. Tomorrow we'll be in the St. Lucie. Nothing to do but steer the boat, fish, sleep, eat, and lie in the sun. All our troubles are over."

"I've been waiting," Nick said. "I didn't know that running away would be such hard work."

"Neither did I," Ben said.

The wind was blowing steadily now from the northwest.

"Let's get sail on this boat and get along," Ben said.

Chapter 9

T THREE-THIRTY in the morning on Thursday the black sloop, *Lion's Paw*, sails set to an easterly wind, disappeared from the Atlantic Ocean. Silently ghosting before the wind, it sailed past the sleeping town of Stuart, Florida, cleared the railway bridge, and turned down the south fork of the St. Lucie River. With Ben at the tiller, Nick hauled in on the jib and mainsail sheets at the turn and, with wind now abeam, they passed Palm City and steered for the entrance to the canal marked by the flashing green number 33 buoy. It was still raining, but the wind was steady and strong.

As they passed the buoy, its green light watery through the rain, the sides of the canal closed in on them until, in the darkness, it looked to Nick as though he could jump ashore without even getting his feet wet. This closeness of the land disturbed him.

THE LION'S PAW

"This would be a good place for your Uncle Pete to catch us," Nick said.

Ben shook his head, the sou'wester throwing a spray of water from the brim. "Don't think so. At least I don't if Uncle Pete has the memory he's always bragging about. Because once we were talking about coming through the St. Lucie and we had to show Uncle Pete that this boat drew too much water and couldn't get through. But they've dredged it recently and it's deep enough now. But I don't think he knows that. I certainly hope he doesn't."

"Me too," Nick said. "There's no place to run to in here."

"We'll hide again in a little while. There's another creek like the one we were in down about eight miles. We'll sneak up there, stay all day, and start out again tomorrow night."

Nick nodded solemnly, his hatbrim spilling water on the face of the binnacle. "Won't we ever be able to sail some in the daytime?" he asked. "Me and Penny aren't used to staying up all night all the time."

"Neither am I," Ben said. "I'm no owl. But I figure we've got two more nights of it. Tomorrow will be a brute. We've got more than sixty miles to do tomorrow to get through the lake—that'll mean sailing from sundown to sunup. The next night won't be so bad—about fifty miles to Fort Myers and the Gulf. Then—we're free."

"Will it rain all the way?" Nick asked.

"Hope not," Ben said. "I've been wet so long the water's soaking through my skin."

"I don't mind the water so much," Nick said. "What I mind is the shivering. My bones are about worn out from shivering. But anyway I won't have to take a bath for maybe a couple of months, will I, Ben?"

"Matters of minor discipline I'll leave up to Penny," Ben said.

Nick looked at Ben's face under the brim of the sou'-wester. "Oh, well," he said. Then he brightened. "But it won't be like taking a bath at the eganahpro. I won't have to stand in line waiting for an open shower with people flicking at me with towels. Did anybody ever flick at you with a towel, Ben?"

"With wet ones," Ben said.

"Me too! There was an eganap who could flick flies off the wall. I saw him one time flick a cockroach right off the ceiling. I had to give him two marbles not to flick me. Everybody gave him something not to flick them, but sometimes he'd forget and flick you anyway, or he'd say what you had given him wasn't enough and he'd flick at you until you gave him something else. He had a lot of things."

"Sounds like a bully," Ben said.

"He was," Nick said. "Nobody liked him, but it wasn't a good idea to tell him that. He'd beat up on you. He was beating up on me one time in the courtyard, but Penny saw him. Don't ever get in a fight with her—she's

129

terrible!" Nick's voice sounded respectful. "She scratches and bites and pulls hair and everything. If the monitor hadn't come that day and stopped her she would have made a real mess out of that boy. Don't ever fight with her, Ben."

"I won't," Ben said.

Nick leaned back and stretched out his legs. "How much farther?" he asked.

"Not much. Half an hour. Sleepy?"

"Who, me?" Nick said. "I don't ever get sleepy."

"Well, I do," Ben said. "Take over, mate, while I get sail off this vessel." Ben suddenly whistled like a boatswain and said, in his deepest voice, "Reeeee-lieve the watch."

Nick took the tiller and steered straight down the middle of the canal. When Ben let the halyard of the mainsail fly, folds of it fell down over Nick, completely covering him. He fought his way out from under the wet canvas and then, steering with his knee the way he had seen Ben do, he helped furl the sail around the boom. When Ben furled the jib the sloop drifted to a stop. Ben came aft and started the engine.

"Won't somebody hear it?" Nick asked.

"Nothing but 'gators and frogs," Ben said. "This is lonesome country through here. Nothing but swamp and scrub oak."

"I want to catch a 'gator, Ben," Nick said. "I really do. I never have even seen one—a live one."

"If it stops raining we'll go after one tomorrow," Ben said, "*after* I've slept a little."

"Will you go, Ben?"

"We'll all go."

"Oh, good!" Nick said. "If you go we'll get one."

"Maybe."

Then the long night ended. Ben turned the boat up into a little winding creek on the north side of the canal. High spoil banks hid them from the mouth of the creek. With the engine stopped, Ben let her drift in silence for a few yards, then dropped the anchor into the soft mud bottom. He let out enough scope to keep from dragging but not enough for her to swing her stern into the shore in case the wind changed. For a while he stood in the bow watching the boat nosing into the wind and feeling the anchor chain with his hands. Satisfied, he went aft, turned out the binnacle light, and put the canvas cover over it, and then he went below.

In the main cabin Nick was already undressing in the dark. Ben leaned close to him and whispered, "I'm going to put something on Penny's hands."

"What?" Nick asked.

"Some medicine. She's probably got some broken blisters." Ben went into his cabin and came back with a bottle and some cotton. Tiptoeing over to Penny's bunk, he knelt down beside it and gently turned one of her hands palm up. He soaked the cotton in the medicine and let it drip down into the palm. He was careful not to touch her flesh with the cotton.

The other hand was lying beside her cheek, and when Ben started to move it Penny turned half over.

"Blast!" Ben whispered in the dark.

Then Penny turned again, and her hand dropped down on the blanket. Ben dripped the medicine onto it as Nick leaned over his shoulder, trying to see.

"Does it sting?" Nick asked.

"Not much," Ben whispered.

Penny suddenly closed her hand and opened it again. Then she moaned a little. Ben and Nick backed away.

"I'll do it better tomorrow," Ben said. "Good night, Nick."

"Night, Ben," Nick said. Then he added, "You're not going to change your mind?"

"About what?"

" 'Gator hunting," Nick said.

"We'll go," Ben whispered.

"Do you think we'll catch any?"

"Go to sleep," Ben said, and went on to his cabin forward.

A few minutes after Nick got into bed a whole battery of frogs opened up simultaneously along the banks of the creek, making such a racket that Nick sat straight up in bed. There were little frogs and huge frogs, and each one of them made a different noise, but after a while he got used to them. Just before he went to sleep some big animal barked. It wasn't like a dog's bark—it was a hollow, almost coughing noise and sounded mean. Nick

wondered for a moment what sort of animal could make
a noise like that. Then he wondered if 'gators made noise.
But the boat around him seemed to protect and shelter
him and he went to sleep.

On the *Lion's Paw* not a hand stirred until after one
o'clock in the afternoon. Penny woke up first. For a while
she lay on her back looking up at the varnished overhead.
Sunlight was pouring down through the glass, and three
flies buzzed endlessly, flying into the beams of sunlight
and looking shiny and clean in them, then flying out and
disappearing. The boat was motionless in the still water
of the creek, and outside it birds were squawking or sing-
ing or just making noise.

Penny moved, and every muscle in her body protested.
Her neck was so stiff she could hardly turn her head; her
shoulder muscles felt as solid as planks, and even the
muscles in her feet were stiff.

Penny managed to roll over. The cabin was a mess. Her
own clothes were lying where she had stepped out of them
in a soggy heap, from which little trickles of water had
run. Nick's sou'wester hat was lying upside down on the
floor; his raincoat was slumped over, rain still on it in
spots, and his clothes (borrowed from Ben) were all over
the place. There were wet footprints everywhere, and
Penny wondered what Ben and Nick had been doing after
she went to sleep to make so many footprints.

Then, without warning, Penny got so hungry she

133

had to swallow. Her stomach felt like a cold toy balloon with no air in it. She got stiffly out of bed, put on the clothes she had worn when she ran away and had washed and let the sun dry the day after they painted the boat.

When she looked at her hands she remembered and felt again the agony of the rowing. Each palm was full of broken blisters, but they didn't hurt as much as she thought they ought to, and when she looked at them more closely she discovered that they had a faint clean smell of pine trees. She wondered, as she began to pick up hers and Nick's wet clothes, if the oar of the dinghy was made out of pine and had made her hands smell that way. She sniffed them again. The scent was faint and very clean.

Tiptoeing, Penny went into the galley and lit the stove. While the coffee began to cook she looked at the rows of cans on the shelves and finally picked out some corned beef. She put some bread on to toast and got the frying pan.

Soon the whole boat began to smell like something to eat. Nick, lying asleep in his bunk, began to wiggle his nose and then to sniff like a dog. When Penny came in to set the table he was still sniffing. He looked funny because he was frowning and sniffing at the same time. Finally his blue eyes opened perfectly wide and looked at her. "I'm hungry," he said.

"Ssssh, you'll wake up Ben."

Nick suddenly leaped out of bed. "What time is it?

134

We've got to go. Where're my clothes? We've got to go. It's late!"

"Go where?"

" 'Gator hunting. 'Gator hunting. Wake up Ben! Where're my clothes?"

"Take it easy, junior," Penny said. "It's not two o'clock yet."

Nick calmed down. With nothing on but his underclothes, he ran out into the galley, gingerly lifted the lid of the coffeepot, and peered into the frying pan. "We ought to have a egg to put on top of that," he said.

"We haven't. All gone. Go get dressed."

"Don't be so bossy," Nick said pleasantly, and disappeared back into the main cabin. In a few seconds he yelled, "Penny!"

"Sssshut up," Penny said, coming to the door.

"All my clothes are wet."

"Your old clothes are on the bookshelf."

"I don't want to wear those," Nick said. "I want to wear Ben's. Those are little-boy clothes."

"You grew up awful fast," Penny remarked. "Maybe Ben will lend you some after he wakes up. But put those on now."

"I'll lend him some now," Ben said from the galley door. "Can't have the crew going around out of uniform."

Ben's hair was tousled all over his head, but he looked rested and happy. He washed his face in the kitchen sink

135

and combed his hair by running his fingers through it.
"You look funny in a dress," he said to Penny.

"Everything else is wet."

Ben went back into his cabin and came out with some
more faded khaki trousers and shirts. "When we get near
Clewiston I'll sneak ashore in the dinghy and get both
of you some clothes."

"I like these all right," Nick said.

"No hand-me-downs for my crew," Ben said. "How're
your hands, Penny?"

"They look worse than they are," she said, showing
him her hands. "And they smell funny."

"Pine oil," Ben said. "We put some on them last
night. We ought to put some more." He got the bottle
and the cotton.

"What is it?" Penny asked as Ben dripped the clear
stuff down on the broken blisters.

"Pine oil from pine trees," Ben said. "Dad says it's the
best disinfectant in the world. He uses it for everything.
It kills ticks, keeps mosquitoes and sand flies away, heals
cuts and blisters, red bugs hate it, and it doesn't sting."

"Is it better than Mercurochrome?" Nick asked.

"Dad says he would just as soon use red ink as that
stuff."

"Didn't I even wake up?" Penny asked.

"Almost," Ben said.

"Mmm," Penny said.

After breakfast they got ready to go 'gator hunting. On

the hook end of a boat hook Ben secured a short piece of small stuff and made a sliding noose in it. He explained that they would slip this over the head of an alligator as it slept in the water and jerk it out.

Penny sat in the stern of the dinghy because her hands were no good for rowing. Nick rowed and Ben lay in the bow, the boat hook held out over the water.

"Just row along very slowly," Ben said, whispering, "and don't make any noise."

"All right. But I don't see any 'gators," Nick said.

"They're hard to see. Look like logs," Ben answered.

The banks of the creek were jungly-looking, with mud going up under the trees. Vines and creepers, Spanish moss and ferns were so thick that the sun could hardly get through, so that everything had a dim, misty green color. In the creek itself were cypress butts, sunken and floating logs, and growing bushes. Ben whispered at intervals, "Pull left," or "Pull right," so that the dinghy wouldn't hit anything.

At last Ben whispered lower than ever, "Stop," and Nick rested on his oars, not lifting them from the water, so they couldn't drip and make a noise.

"There's one up beside that log," Ben whispered. "See him?"

Nick turned and peered ahead. A big log, with the bark peeled off in places, was lying half on the bank, half in the water. Beside it, like another log, was something which didn't look much like what Nick thought an alligator looked like. "Is that it?" he whispered, pointing with his elbow.

Ben nodded.

"Let's go get it then," Nick said.

"Look at it some more," Ben said.

Nick studied the thing lying beside the log. Slowly he began to see a raised hump, then the long back. Finally he could see the scales and spines and a long line of little dots that marked the tail. On the other end there were two little knobs sticking out of the water, and ahead of them the snout of the animal.

"I can see everything but his feet now," Nick whispered. "Do you want me to row up to it?"

"If you don't mind, just row the other way," Ben whispered back. "And row very quietly. That 'gator is a good deal bigger than this dinghy. Just one wallop of his tail and we'd be floating around in a bunch of splinters. . . . Go way around him and don't wake him up."

As Nick began to row slowly and cautiously he felt a little scared and looked up at Penny. She was staring at the sleeping alligator, her eyes wide open and her mouth open a little also. Nick felt better—he wasn't, he decided, half as scared as she was.

In a little while Ben said, "Slow down—real slow."

Nick hardly moved the oars through the water. Turning, he saw, lying beside a clump of green bushes, another line of scales, another snout.

"How big is that one?" Nick whispered.

138

THE LION'S PAW

"Two-three feet. Just right. Go right up behind him."

As Nick rowed slowly toward the alligator his breath began to flutter in his throat and his stomach felt as though it were trying to turn a complete flip but not quite making it.

The boat glided slowly toward the 'gator. Ben shifted his weight with infinite care and stretched the boat hook out as far as he could, the open noose hanging just above the water.

In an almost inaudible whisper Ben finally said, "Stop."

Then the boat drifted. Nick, turned half around, stared at the scales showing above water and at the curved line of little humps along the top of the tail. In one of the little knobs at the head he suddenly saw an eye—dim yellow, with a black slit covered with a sort of film.

Ben raised the hanging noose an inch, and as the boat drifted on the noose traveled up the back of the 'gator, passed the two eye knobs and the two little nostrils above the water.

Slowly, slowly then, as the boat drifted to a stop, Ben began to lower the noose. At first the thin rope floated on the water, and Nick could hear his heart beating and wondered why the noise it was making didn't scare everything around there. Then the rope sank slowly down through the clear water, and when the noose was half under water Ben started pulling it carefully back.

Then, swooping down from a tree, a long-legged little

bird with a little round body banked in its flight and landed on the alligator's back.

The film over the yellow eye slid slowly open, and the eye appeared clean, yellow, and baleful. Then the film closed again and the bird walked up and down the alligator's back, pecking with a long, thin beak at the hard scales. It paid no attention whatsoever to the boat hook or the dinghy.

Ben began again drawing the noose down around the long jaws. Under the clear water now Nick could see the long snout of the thing and the feet on short little legs lying peacefully floating. He was so close to it now that he could see where the nostrils blew air out in a little path on the water and he could see the white line of the noose slowly coming back along the head.

Then Ben whispered, "Stand by," and lifted up suddenly on the boat hook, at the same time sliding back onto his knees in the bottom of the dinghy.

For a second all remained peaceful and silent except for the humming of bugs and the song of birds. Then the alligator exploded into action. As the noose slid up and clamped around the back of his jaws, lifting his head up, he thrashed straight up out of the water, fell with a splash, began to swim in violent circles and then to roll over and over, winding the rope up until the boat hook was drawn down against his face. His violence threw muddy water all over them, and his opening and shutting jaws tried to bite the dinghy and the boat hook.

Ben slowly maneuvered the raging thing back alongside the boat, where its tail hammered at the curved bilges. Suddenly, when the 'gator's mouth snapped shut with a wet smack, Ben reached down with his bare hand and grabbed it by the snout.

"Get his tail! Grab it!" Ben yelled at Nick.

Nick peered down at the tail thrashing around in the water and wondered if Ben had lost his mind. Nobody could grab that thing—not and hold on.

"Grab it by the end," Ben yelled as he wrestled with his end, still gripping the snout.

Nick leaned out of the dinghy, his arms reaching down for the long tail, dodging it when it came flailing at him through the air. But for a split second the 'gator lay still and Nick grabbed the tail with both hands.

He never knew exactly what happened after that. He remembered the feel of the tail—hard and bony, the scales slick. Then he remembered the tail moving, and he might as well have been holding the end of a PT boat.

With water flying all around, Penny only saw that Nick was in the boat, reaching down, one second and then flying out of the boat and falling down on top of the 'gator the next.

Nick landed half astride of the animal, which immediately began to flail around worse than ever. The tail caught him on the side of the head and knocked him up against the dinghy, and then the 'gator half swam and half walked up on top of Nick and shoved him down under the muddy water.

141

THE LION'S PAW

Ben turned loose the snout and grabbed the boat hook. Throwing his weight onto it, he shoved the 'gator away from the boat with one hand and with the other he reached down and grabbed Nick by the top of his pants. With Penny helping, they heaved Nick back into the boat and dumped him sprawling into the bottom.

With the rope slack for a second the 'gator snapped his jaws on it once, cut it cleanly off, and swam away, his body making a hump in the water as he went.

Suddenly everything was peaceful and quiet again. Ben said, "Blast! He got away," and Nick sat up slowly and spat water into the creek, then wiped the muddy water off his face. When he could see again there was nothing to show that an alligator had been around there except a muddy splotch which slowly spread.

Nick looked at Ben. Ben grinned a little and fished the boat hook out of the water. Nick got up on the thwart and pushed the oars out. He looked at Penny and she looked back at him with wide blue eyes.

Nick's ears were still ringing from the blow from the tail, and he was soaked with muddy water.

Nick glared at Penny. "You think I'm scared, don't you?" he demanded.

Penny shook her head.

Nick rowed a few strokes, then stopped. "How was I to know he was so strong?" he asked angrily. "Nobody told me he was so strong."

"He just got you off balance, Nick," Ben said.

"Somebody should have told me he was so strong," Nick declared. He pulled the oars in and turned around to face Ben. "If he was so strong how did you hold his snout?"

"His tail is much stronger than his head," Ben said. "You did all right, Nick."

"Well—he got away," Nick said. "We'll have to find another one, I guess."

"They'll all be gone now after all that racket," Ben said. He came aft and told Nick he would row back to the boat. Nick moved to sit down beside Penny.

"I don't see how you held his jaws that way," Nick said after a while.

"They have a one-way bite," Ben said. "Nothing could keep their jaws from shutting, but after they're shut you could hold one's mouth shut with two fingers."

"Oh," Nick said.

Ben rowed awhile in silence. Then he said, "Well, Nick, do you still want to catch a 'gator?"

Nick looked at him, remembering the smack of the tail. "Sure," Nick said. "You think I'm scared, don't you?"

Ben shook his head slowly. "Not you," he said.

"Well, I'm not," Nick said. "Not much, anyway."

143

FTER SUPPER, as they waited for darkness, they sat in the cockpit, studying the chart of the St. Lucie Canal and the Caloosahatchee Canal and River.

Ben said, "We've got to get this navy organized better. The way it is, with everybody working at the same time or sleeping, if we got a long spell of three or four days, all hands would collapse at the same time. Starting tonight we'll stand regular watches. Nick, from here to Lake Okeechobee is eighteen miles. With this wind it'll take four hours to get there. That'll be your watch—you'll steer while Penny and I sleep."

"You mean, all by myself?" Nick asked. "With the sails up and everything?"

Ben nodded. "The wind's just right, Nick. All you'll

144

have to do is keep smack in the middle of the canal. There's nothing to it."

"Suppose something happens?" Nick asked.

"Give me a buzz," Ben said. "But I don't think anything will happen."

"All right," Nick said a little dubiously.

Ben went on: "The lake is tricky, so I'll sail her across that. Then, when we get back into the canal on the other side of the lake, Penny'll take over and sail her the rest of the way. That'll mean that tonight Nick and I get the heavy end and Penny has a short watch. But tomorrow night we'll change around. Penny'll take the first watch and Nick and I'll have short ones."

"How will I know when I've gone far enough?" Penny asked.

Ben pointed to the chart. "We've got to get to Lake Hicpochee before dawn. When you get to this flashing red buoy you'll be about a mile from the lake. You can wake me up then."

Penny's voice was much weaker than Nick's had been as she said, "All right."

"Let's get going," Ben said, getting up.

Penny had said good night a long time ago and Ben had said it before she did. Nick, sitting in the cockpit, looked around the silent topsides of the boat. Above him the sails were set for the wind almost astern, the moon was halfway up the sky, and through the sails it made

145

a sort of luminous glow. Sometimes, when Nick just looked at the cockpit, it felt as though the boat wasn't moving at all, but when he looked out at the close banks of the canal he saw the dark trees, the spoil banks, the bushes sliding rapidly past and he could hear the whisper of water at the bow of the sloop.

He had got over the first fear which had held him almost rigid at the tiller. Now he leaned back, looked up at the moon and the clear stars in the faintly glowing sky, looked at the black thin lines of the shrouds, the puffs of baggy wrinkle on them to keep the sails from rubbing the bare wires.

Nick began to think about the alligator again. He smiled a little in the darkness as he thought about how scared he had been but how he hadn't let Penny and Ben know about it.

Then slowly Nick began to get mad about the alligator. He felt humiliated that he had let a little alligator flip him out of the dinghy and get him all wet and muddy and slap him with its tail. Who did that alligator think he was, anyhow?

Nick decided that no alligator was going to get away with a thing like that. Tomorrow, when they hid again, he'd go show those alligators that they couldn't slap him with their tails. He'd show 'em.

Nick began to wonder how far he had gone. He believed that he had been steering the boat for at least four hours, and maybe it was time to wake up Ben. Maybe he was already out in the lake. But he wasn't—the banks of the canal were still sliding silently past.

Nick got up and, holding the tiller with just the tips of his fingers, he leaned forward as far as he could and tried to make out what time it was on the luminous face of the clock hanging in the companionway. The blurred greenish hands looked as though they pointed to a quarter to nine, but Nick knew that it must be much later than that. Maybe the clock had stopped. He'd tell Ben about it when he woke him up.

He settled back on the cushions of the cockpit. "Things were getting better," he decided. At first he hadn't been sure that running away was all he had thought it ought to be. He remembered the long walk from Mrs. Wertz's farm and then the longer walk with Penny from the orphanage to Ben's boat. That first night had been miserable, with him and Penny in the dinghy getting so cold and wet. Every night had been bad except this one. They never did sleep the way he was used to sleeping. But now it was better. In a little while—maybe less than an hour—he could go to bed. When he woke up it would be broad daylight. All he would have to do would be to wash his face and then eat.

But things were going to get even better later on. When they got to Captiva Island and began looking for the Lion's Paw—that's when things would really be good. Nick wondered what it would be like under the sea with the face mask on. Maybe Ben would teach him how to swim—really swim—not just pretend you were swimming while your feet were still on bottom.

"It must be time to wake up Ben," he thought. He got up and looked at the clock again. It hadn't stopped because the hands now looked like nine o'clock. But it wasn't running right, because if it was really only nine o'clock that would mean he had two more hours to steer, and he knew that he had already steered for at least four hours. The clock was all out of whack.

After a while Nick decided that he should practice steering with his eyes closed. Maybe when it was a very dark night he would have to steer, and he ought to practice steering without being able to see anything.

Nick closed his eyes and listened. Nothing happened. He opened them again and saw that the boat was still gliding straight down the middle of the canal. He closed his eyes again. The movement of his eyelids going down seemed to pull his head down also. He tried that, opening and closing his eyes and letting his head go down until his chin rested on his chest. The boat stayed right in the middle of the channel.

"I'll do it for a long time," Nick said to himself, and closed his eyes again. For a few seconds the lids trembled a little with his effort to keep them closed, then they stopped trembling and began to feel peaceful and heavy. His chin on his chest felt like a little warm spot, and the stretching of his neck muscles felt good. His eyelids got heavier and heavier, and he began to breathe slowly and deeply.

148

THE LION'S PAW

When Nick slowly opened his eyes there was no longer a path of golden moonlight stretching out ahead of the boat. Instead there was a black wall toward which the boat was rushing.

An ice-cold shiver swept over him as he realized that the boat was driving straight toward the bank of the canal. Looking wildly around, Nick found the path of moonlight far away and, beyond it, the other bank. He slammed the tiller all the way over, and the black wall slid away; the sails rattled a little above him, then filled with wind again.

Sweat popped out on Nick's forehead and lip, and he could feel it between his shoulders as he steadied the boat in the middle of the canal again.

He had almost been asleep. "Asleep on watch," he thought. He remembered in the orphanage school a story the teacher had read about a sailor sleeping on watch and how he had to be shot at sunrise. The icy chill went up and down his backbone again, and he looked anxiously down the dark companionway to see if Ben or Penny had seen him. The companionway was empty, and Nick sighed and relaxed against the cushions. He decided that he would never again close his eyes while he was steering. He wouldn't even blink them. And if something —a bug or something—flew into his eye he would just let it stay there; he wouldn't close his eye no matter how much it hurt.

Nick sat without blinking until his eyes got dry and began to burn. Staring straight at the path of moonlight, it began to swim around and then to jerk like flames in a fireplace. When he blinked, his eyes got all right and the path settled down. Nick decided that it was all right to blink, but not too many times and always as fast as he could.

By the time the clock struck six bells Nick was so sleepy that he had to keep standing up. Whenever he sat down on the cushion something seemed to pour down on him —something like darkness, except that it was warm and close and heavy. It seemed to lift him up into a warm softness and rock him until it was impossible not to go to sleep. With one hand on the tiller he would walk as far as he could one way, then walk the other way. He would stand with the tiller between his knees and steer that way, or he would sit on the sharp coaming of the cockpit and steer with his bare toes.

After a long, long time Nick began to worry. Would it be possible, he wondered, had it ever happened, as long as anybody could remember, that the sun had not come up when it was supposed to? That it just stayed night all night and then all day and then all night again? Maybe that's what had happened now, he worried. Maybe he had been steering all night long and now the sun wasn't going to come up and he would go right on steering all through the day, except that the day would be just as dark as night.

Nick felt with his finger tips for the two little buttons for the buzzers. The right one rang in Ben's cabin, the

150

left one in the main cabin. Maybe, he thought, he ought to ring them both if this was going to be a day when the sun wasn't coming up.

Then, far down the path of moonlight, he saw a white light. The instant he saw it it went out.

"Maybe," Nick thought, "that's the sun trying to come up."

The light came on again—white and clear—then went off.

When it came on again it was much closer, and Nick suddenly realized that that was the buoy Ben had told him about. It was the entrance to Lake Okeechobee.

The long watch was over.

The clock struck eight bells just as Nick rang the buzzer in Ben's cabin. Ben appeared almost immediately and he was already dressed.

"How you making, Nick?" Ben asked as he came into the cockpit.

"I think I see the light," Nick said.

"Yep." Ben stood up, put his bare heels together, and saluted. "I relieve you, sir," he said. "Sleepy?"

"Me!" Nick said. "Well—good night, Ben."

"Night."

Nick didn't even remember going down the companion ladder or getting into bed.

Ben took his departure from the buoy and steered by compass toward the next one. Out on the lake it was almost like being at sea, except that the water was barely riffled by the wind. The *Lion's Paw* flew along, the sails taut and curved, the bow wave whispering to the ship. Ben adjusted the sheets in half-inch lengths and settled down, feeling the good movement of the boat, enjoying the feel of freedom it had as the warm wind drove it farther and farther from the places where his uncle would be looking for him.

This was the first time since they had started on the long voyage that Ben had had time to sit for a little while in peace and think. He remembered the car lights on the wharf, the yelling of his uncle, and the useless blowing of the car horn as the *Hard A Lee* had pulled out and swung away from the lights of the city, pointing her bow toward the dark and open sea.

So much had happened since then and he tried to count the days they had been gone, but he couldn't remember them all. The number of days wasn't an important thing, he decided.

Ben thought of the two orphans. They were all right, he decided. Neither one of them had whimpered a single time, and they had both taken a whale of a beating. They were good shipmates.

What was going to happen to them? he wondered. And then he stopped. There was no use wondering yet, he decided. As each day came they would work it out. When his father came, then would be the time to decide.

When? When? And—was he ever coming? Was he

even still alive? Ben thought of the ships he had read about which had been sunk in the Pacific. He remembered reading about two men—he thought it was on the carrier *Yorktown*—who had been trapped down inside the ship. They could talk to the outside of the sinking ship by telephone, but they couldn't get out themselves. On the telephone, even while they knew that they would never get out, they had cracked jokes. They had played acey-deucy while the ship sank.

Ben thought of what it must have been like for those two men trapped down inside of a watertight compartment in the bottom of the ship. After a while, as the ship slowly sank, the air must have become very bad. Then, probably just getting dimmer and dimmer or maybe going out all of a sudden, the lights must have failed and left them in utter darkness. It must have been very silent down there with the ship going down to the bottom now, the sea marked with oil where she had been. And water must have broken in on them after a while—maybe just a little at a time—maybe just a trickle coming across the floor toward where they were playing acey-deucy. Maybe when they saw the water they had stopped for a second the shaking of the dice in the cup, the moving of the little round pieces on the board, and had looked up at each other. Maybe they had grinned. Maybe they had had to look down again so that each one wouldn't see into the other one's eyes.

Was that the way his father had been trapped? But Ben

153

didn't believe it. His father was big and fast-moving and powerful. Nothing could have trapped him in a ship. If he had to do it, he would have broken through steel to get out. He couldn't die that way—trapped and forsaken, slowly drowning.

What had happened to him? When the ship went down did he swim away from it? He had written in a letter that he always wore a Mae West when they were in enemy water. Had he been hurt by the torpedo or whatever it was that had sunk the ship? Had he been so badly hurt that he had died, floating around helplessly, held up by the Mae West, the green dye marker spreading a lovely iridescent circle around him? Had it been night or day? Or had he just lived for days and nights floating in the empty sea with no food, no water, and the screeching sea gulls flying around and around waiting for him to die? Had sharks or barracuda got him?

Where was he? Was he dead? Somebody must know. Somebody on his ship must have seen him. He was big and people liked him—somebody must have seen a big man. . . . Maybe somebody had seen him; maybe they had told the Navy what they had seen—that he was dead.

But he wasn't. Ben's fingers on the tiller tightened. He wasn't dead. Somewhere—on the sea or in the jungle out there or on some little island no one even knew existed— his father was still alive.

Ben wished that there was something he could do to help his father get back. Just waiting was hard; feeling so helpless and empty all the time made him want to fight. But there was nothing he could do except wait some more —month after month.

Then Ben thought of the Lion's Paw. Somehow that sea shell had become a great deal more than just a sea shell. Somehow it had become the only thing he could do to help his father; to go and find a Lion's Paw would— somehow—bring him back.

A thought as clear and sharp as broken ice suddenly flashed into Ben's mind. "When I find the shell he'll come back." That was all there was to the thought.

"When I find the shell he'll come back."

The clock struck two bells, and Lake Okeechobee had been crossed, the new canal banks were beside him, the sleeping town of Moore Haven was behind him, and there were only a few more miles to Lake Hicpochee. "Let Penny sleep," he thought.

As dawn came false in the eastern sky Ben steered the boat out of the canal and felt his way along through the mists rising from the water of the lake. Sailing at last into a little tributary as far from the canal as he could get, he dropped anchor quietly and furled the sails. He was tired as he went slowly down the ladder forward and into his little cabin.

In the light of dawn he looked at the dim picture of his father above his bed. It was a picture he had taken while his father was at the tiller. His father was grinning, a pipe held in his teeth. He was wearing a shirt, torn at the shoulder, and a floppy old canvas hat. He hadn't shaved that day, and the sunlight showed the stubble on his chin.

Ben climbed wearily into bed and looked up at the picture. "Good night, Skipper," he said, whispering.

Chapter 11

HEN Penny woke up it was broad daylight. For a little while she lay in bed wondering why Ben hadn't waked her, then she began to fear that something had gone wrong. She jumped out of bed, glanced at Nick sound asleep in his bunk, and, putting on her clothes, ran up the companion ladder.

It was a beautiful day. The sloop was anchored, as usual, in a little hidden creek so that the jungly growth, clean and green in the sunlight, was close to it. As Penny came out on deck seven white herons rose in silent flight and glided away, their long legs streaming out behind them. Penny noticed that the sails were furled, everything shipshape.

She felt a little angry at Ben as she went below again.

157

THE LION'S PAW

He should have waked her up and let her stand her watch the way they had agreed. He must have stayed at the tiller almost all night. Penny also had a little feeling of guilt because, for the first time since they had run away, she felt wonderful. Every day up until now she had felt tired or hurt in one place or another—her feet after the long walk, her hands after the rowing. But this morning she felt wonderful all over after a whole night's sleep.

Penny cooked and ate her breakfast and afterward, being as quiet as she could, she made some biscuits because all the loaf bread they had started with was gone. By the time she got the biscuits done Nick woke up and, a little while later, Ben.

"There's a town a few miles from here," Ben said. "I'm going up there this morning and get some gear. How big are you, Nick?"

Nick looked surprised. "Not very," he said.

"I mean how big around? I want to get you and Penny some clothes."

"Not short pants!" Nick said.

"Anything I can get," Ben said. "Maybe just overalls."

"Anything but short pants," Nick said.

"How about you, Penny?"

"I don't know," Penny said. "But I'd like overalls too. They're cheaper than dresses."

Ben got a flexible steel tape out of the toolbox and measured Penny and Nick around the waist and down the leg. He wrote the measurements on a piece of paper.

158

THE LION'S PAW

Sitting at the table, Ben rapped on it with his knuckles and spoke to an invisible somebody. "Orderly," he said, "present my compliments to the supply officer and request that he report to my stateroom—immediately."

Nick looked around for the orderly.

"Do we need anything, Penny?" Ben asked.

"Bread—unless we're going to bake it ourselves."

Ben wrote that down.

"Do you want us to do anything while you're gone?" Penny asked.

Ben shook his head. "If anybody comes snooping around, tell them that this boat belongs to your—brother, and that he'll be right back."

As Ben started out Nick put on an innocent expression and said, "Ben, can I go rowing in the dinghy while you're gone? I want to practice."

"Go ahead," Ben said.

Nick rowed Ben over to the bank and then went back to the *Lion's Paw*. Penny leaned over and told him not to row out on the lake where someone might see him, and Nick said, "Do you think I'm crazy?"

Nick rowed innocently around as long as Penny was on deck, but as soon as she went below he changed course and started purposefully up the creek. In the bottom of the dinghy he had stowed a boat hook and, concealed in his pocket, he had a length of rope with which to make a noose. Nick had a very determined look in his eye.

Soon the winding creek hid him from the sloop, and

the water was shallow enough so that he could stand up in the stern and pole the boat along with the boat hook. As Ben had done, he went very slowly and silently and kept watching for alligators.

In a little while he saw one lying in the mud of the bank. Nick almost turned right around and went back, for the 'gator was ten feet long, and as he went past it turned its head and looked at him with the clear pale yellow eyes. It opened its jaws wide, and Nick could see the rows of long teeth and the white, flabby-looking inside of its mouth.

Farther on he saw another one, but it was big, too, and as soon as he got close to it it waddled slowly down across the muddy bank and slid into the water. For a little while he could see where it was going by the hump it made in the water and the trail of mud, but finally it disappeared altogether.

He saw three more, but they all slid off into the water before he could get near them. At last he was so far up the little creek that there was hardly room enough for the dinghy to move, and when it finally stopped, stuck in the mud, Nick stood for a moment half disappointed and half relieved. He had to admit that he was a little afraid of the alligators, especially hunting them this way all by himself. Maybe he ought to go get Penny to help him.

Nick pushed the dinghy out of the mud and turned it around, then as he started to go back he saw, in the mud of the bank, some tracks. They weren't like the others he had seen, which had had big, sloppy footprints on each side of a wavy slick line where the alligator's tail dragged. These were little. The footprints were clear where the toes dug into the mud, and the line the tail made between them was just a slick place on the mud.

The footprints went away from the creek.

Looking around to be sure that there were no big ones watching him, Nick pushed the bow of the dinghy into the mudbank and climbed out. He sank into mud almost to his knees, but as he followed the little claw marks the mud got better—down to his ankles. He lost the little track in some leaves, then found it again further on. In one place the alligator had just wandered around, but then it had started on again.

Nick followed the tracks until they led him to a little pool of water left by the rain. As he came toward it he at last saw the alligator as it slid down into the water. It was about eight inches long, and its scales, unlike those of the big ones, were clean and yellow with blackish spots on them.

Nick slogged his way to the edge of the pool and looked down into the inch-deep water. The alligator had made a curving line of mud out to the middle of the pool, but there it ended in a little cloud of muddy water.

Around him the woods were silent. Far away, in a circle, Nick could hear things—bugs and birds and a squirrel—but right where he was there wasn't a sound and nothing moved, not even the little green leaves at the tops of the trees.

Nick looked all around to be sure that no big alligators were watching him; then, going very slowly and trying his best not to muddy the water, he waded out into the little pool. He stopped a foot or so from the last trace of the alligator and waited, standing perfectly still, until the mud he and the 'gator had made settled like wet brown dust to the bottom.

Looking down through the clear water now, he could see where the little alligator had gone under the mud. It had made an outline of its body in the smooth mud, so that he could see where its head was, and there was a thin line marking the tail.

Very carefully Nick reached down, his fingers open and ready to grab. Nothing moved; nothing made a sound. As his fingers touched the surface of the water and slid down into it Nick held his breath. As his fingers touched the mud he suddenly shoved down hard and grabbed.

He had it. Through the oozing mud in his hand he felt the rounded body thrashing back and forth.

Jerking his hand out, he held the muddy alligator up as its little feet on the short legs clawed uselessly at his hand and its little mouth opened and snapped shut as fast as it could, the yellow eyes, clear of mud, blazing at him. Nick was surprised by the grunting noise the little 'gator made.

162

THE LION'S PAW

Holding the 'gator tightly, Nick washed him off in the pool and then, feeling jubilant, he began slogging his way back to the dinghy. The alligator kept on grunting.

He had almost reached the boat and was floundering in mud up to his knees when he heard the noise behind him. It was a loud, abrupt hissing sound, and he twisted around to see what it was.

Coming toward him through the mud, its pale yellow eyes fixed on him, its body held up clear of the mud on the short legs, was an enormous alligator hissing through the two little nostrils on the end of its bony snout.

For a second Nick stood in the mud, petrified with fear, as the alligator rushed toward him. And then, with all his strength, he plowed toward the dinghy, his legs fighting the clawing mud, his hands and arms waving around to keep him from falling off balance. Once he looked back over his shoulder, and the alligator was moving much faster than he was.

When Nick half fell over into the dinghy the 'gator was only a few feet away and coming fast. Dropping the little alligator, Nick grabbed an oar, shoved the dinghy's bow out of the mud, and swung it downstream. As the big 'gator came hissing down the bank and into the water Nick grabbed the other oar and fitted both of them into the oarlocks. For a moment the alligator disappeared in the muddy water, and as Nick began to row he thought that it had gone. Bracing his feet, he threw all his weight against the oars and the dinghy began to slide away.

Then, behind the dinghy, Nick saw the moving hump of water. At first it was just rounded and smooth, but then it began to stretch out, getting thinner and thinner, and suddenly the 'gator's long head and scaly back broke through the surface, the knobs where the eyes were making two long ripples and its beating tail sending waves of muddy water washing against the bank.

Nick rowed harder. His breath was now dry as dust in his throat and he could hear it rasping back and forth as he tried to breathe. His arms and legs began to feel like bagfuls of water, with no strength in them, and the pumping of his heart felt as though it would break through his ribs.

With easy, powerful strokes of its tail the 'gator gained on him fast, the little eyes sliding toward him and watching him, the hump of the nostrils cutting the water like the bow of a boat.

Nick stopped rowing and grabbed the boat hook, which was of white oak with a handle about six feet long, equipped with a brass fitting on the end which had a spike ending in a little ball and a curved brass hook. Crouching in the stern of the boat, Nick clubbed the boat hook and waited.

The alligator came straight at him, the little eyes baleful and steady, the tail making a swishing noise in the water.

With all his strength Nick brought the boat hook

164

RUSHING TOWARD HIM WAS AN ENORMOUS
ALLIGATOR.

down on the snout, the brass fitting banging the hump where the nostrils opened and making the pole shiver in his hands.

The 'gator disappeared in a mass of foam and mud as it seemed to hump up in the middle and thrash with its whole body. Nick reached for the bottom with the boat hook and leaned all his weight on it, shoving the dinghy fast downstream. He reached again, shoved, jerked the end out of the clinging mud, and shoved again, the water getting deeper and deeper, the dinghy going in sudden leaps and gliding stops.

The alligator appeared suddenly right astern. It came whooshing up through the muddy water, and as it broke the surface it opened its jaws and came for the dinghy.

To Nick it seemed that everything stopped moving except the rushing jaws of the 'gator. The creek, the woods, the sky were silent, and the sunlight made everything crystal-clear. He saw muddy water in the bottom of the dinghy. He saw his little alligator lying motionless but still grunting on the yellow, varnished blade of one of the oars. He saw a turtle, its shell glossy, sitting on a log.

He saw the teeth of the alligator's upper jaw and saw a silver drop of water fall from one of them. The inside of the thing's mouth was soft-looking and dead white and wet and it hung in smooth folds from the top jaw, sagged in the bottom of the mouth. Back where the throat was the white, folding flesh looked as though it were puckered up a little, closing the throat. Muddy water swirled slowly around the lower front teeth.

The gaping jaws seemed to grow bigger and bigger as they swam straight toward him. To Nick the white, tooth-ringed mouth seemed to be huge, engulfing everything.

For long seconds Nick squatted perfectly still in the bilges of the dinghy as the jaws slid swiftly toward him. He couldn't breathe; he couldn't move a muscle as he stared at the jaws.

Then everything broke apart like an explosion. In the woods jay birds began suddenly to screech, the turtle slid with a splash off the log, the little alligator scurried up the side of the dinghy and fell back on the oar. Nick lunged forward with the boat hook and watched the brass fitting, bright in the sunlight, go in between the two jaws, go on until it disappeared into the puckered folds of the white flesh back where the throat was.

The top jaw came down with a crash which tore the boat hook out of his hands and flailed it around, banging it against the dinghy. Again and again and again the jaws opened and crashed shut, sending showers of water away from the head. Then three feet of the handle of the boat hook floated away on the wild water and the alligator began to whirl over and over, its great tail rising from the water and flailing down again, thrashing the stream into a froth of mud and water.

Hanging on with both hands to the wildly pitching dinghy, Nick got back to the thwart, shoved the oars

168

out, and began to row. Sweat and muddy water streamed into his eyes; he rammed the boat against the bank, backed it off, and went ahead again. He was half blind, but he could still hear the thrashing of the alligator.

Missing a stroke, Nick clawed the sweat and water out of his eyes and looked up the creek. The beast was still whirling around and around, its back thrusting up for a moment, then its white, smooth belly, the little legs clawing the empty air, then the back again. He could hear the squashy snapping of the jaws as they opened and shut.

When he was fifty feet from the *Lion's Paw* Nick began to yell for Penny. Rowing wildly, the dinghy's wake like a crazy snake in the water, he yelled at the top of his lungs and kept on yelling even after he had heard Penny answering him.

Then, when the dinghy bumped into the side of the sloop, Nick collapsed. He turned loose the oars, and one of them slid out of the oarlock and floated away.

"Nick, what's the matter? What's the matter?" Penny asked, her voice full of fear as she leaned over the side of the sloop.

"Alligator—got—me," Nick said between pants. "Big—jaws—bite—chased—me—boat—hook right in two."

"What? What?" Penny asked.

Nick took a deep breath and looked up into the frightened face of his sister. "I said a 'gator got me," he said.

"How? Where?" Penny asked, her voice rising.

Nick let the breath out and tried to stand up, but his

169

knees had gone and he sat down again with a wet thump. "The boat hook's gone," he said in a low voice. "He bit it right in two."

"Nick," Penny said sternly, "get out of that boat and come up here."

"I can't," Nick said. "I haven't got any knees."

"Are you crazy? What happened?"

"An alligator tried to eat the dinghy," Nick said. "While I was in it."

"Oh, Nick!" Penny said. "You ought to have your mouth washed out with soap."

"He bit the boat hook right in two. He's back there now, going around and around."

"Really?" Penny said, her voice low.

"He was huge," Nick said. "He was as long as the *Lion's Paw*, and his mouth was white inside."

"Is he coming?"

Nick shook his head. "I fixed him. I put the boat hook all the way down his throat."

"Nick, *please* get out of that boat and tell me what happened."

"All right." Nick retrieved the floating oar and then, as he was about to climb out, he remembered the little alligator. It had disappeared, and he began frantically searching for it in the bilge water and under the oars.

"What's the matter now?" Penny asked.

"I've lost my alligator."

Penny straightened up and looked down into the

dinghy. "Nick, what's the matter with you?" she asked slowly.

Then Nick found the little alligator far up in the bow. When he got it by the tail it whipped around and tried to bite him. He grabbed it with his other hand and held it up.

"See?" he said.

Penny looked at the little alligator in amazement. "You really did," she said slowly.

After Penny and Nick had got the dinghy cleaned out, the alligator in a basin with some water in it, and Nick had removed some of the mud, the story about the alligator had been told five times. And when Ben came back in the afternoon it had to be told two or three times more, and finally all three of them went back up the creek to see where it had happened. Nick, who was afraid that maybe they didn't believe all of it, was happier after they found the end of the boat hook, the oak handle chewed through.

They found nothing else.

Back on the sloop, the dinghy upside down abaft the mast, Ben showed them the stuff he had bought. Overalls—stiff and new—some cotton shirts, a straw hat for each one of them, and some underclothes. Then from another paper package he unfolded two cotton nightgowns with little birds printed on them.

"These are yours," he said to Penny. "Nick, here're some pajamas for you."

Penny retired to the galley to try on first her night-gowns and then the shirts and overalls. The nightgowns were just right, but the other things were too big.

"They'll shrink plenty," Ben said.

He had also bought two combs, some toothbrushes and powder, some high-smelling soap in cakes shaped like animals, and some towels.

After supper, as they sat around waiting for dark, Ben pulled out a torn piece of newspaper. "They're still after us," he said. "I noticed this in a paper and swiped it."

" 'RUNAWAY CHILDREN DISAPPEAR,' " Ben read the headline.

"The three children—two of them escaped orphans—who ran away in a sailboat have disappeared, according to Mr. Peter Lanford of this city. Six days ago Mr. Lanford's nephew, Benjamin R. Sturges, 15, the son of the well-known yacht builder, Lieutenant Ben Sturges, who was killed while on active duty in the Navy, ran away in Lieutenant Sturges's sloop, *Hard A Lee*. It is believed he is accompanied by two children—brother and sister—who had escaped from the local orphanage.

"No trace has been found of this sloop, although a coastwise search has been conducted by the Coast Guard, Navy, and Merchant Marine, and Mr. Lanford now fears that the boat may have been wrecked and the children lost.

"Mr. Lanford reports that he has received many false clues to the whereabouts of this boat, and people have reported sighting it as far south as Key West and as far north as Norfolk. Mr. Lanford, who is offering five hun-

172

dred dollars reward, has thoroughly investigated each of these reports but has found them all to be false.

"Anyone knowing or hearing about such a boat, or seeing any of the children, is requested to telephone or wire collect to Mr. Peter Lanford, 2719 Valle Vista Drive, of this city."

Ben crumpled the paper into a ball and threw it up into the cockpit. "I think we've fooled him," Ben said. "It doesn't say a word about searching in the Gulf of Mexico."

"You know," Penny said quietly, "I wish there was some way we could let your Uncle Pete know that we're all right."

"I have," Ben said. "There was a truck at a filling station going to Miami. I wrote a note to one of the boys who used to work with Dad, asking him to tell Uncle Pete that we were all right. The truck driver said he would mail it when he got to Miami."

"Suppose he doesn't?" Penny asked. "Suppose he gets suspicious and opens it?"

"He didn't look very suspicious. He looked sort of dumb. But anyway, even if he opened it and read it, it wouldn't make much sense to him because Dad used to call Uncle Pete 'Sluggo,' and I just said in the note, 'Please tell Sluggo we are all fine and not to worry.' Jimmy will know that I sent it and he'll remember Dad calling Uncle Pete 'Sluggo.' "

"He'll think we're in Miami," Nick said.

173

Ben nodded. "At least I hope he will. Anyhow, if everything goes wrong—the driver gets suspicious, or the man at the filling station or somebody has seen the boat today—it won't make any difference. In an hour we'll be gone. Tomorrow we'll be in the Gulf."

Penny sighed.

Nick said, "What's the Gulf like, Ben?"

"About the same as the Atlantic. Not as rough, and it's more tropical. And there aren't any alligators—not where we're going."

Nick shrugged. "I don't care. I've already got one.'

"It's a wonder he didn't get you," Ben said. "All right, let's get rolling. Penny, you catch the long one tonight—from here to Alva. Nick will take her from Alva to Fort Myers, and I'll take her down to the bay."

The *Lion's Paw*, in the cover of darkness, ghosted out of Lake Hicpochee and turned west again toward the Gulf of Mexico and, they thought, the end of being pursued.

Chapter 12

HE *Lion's Paw* was no longer con-
fined between the close banks of a canal, her keel no
longer barely cleared the earth of a channel, her bows no
longer sliced out curling waves of water tinged yellow
with mud. She was sailing full and by to a westerly wind
across San Carlos Bay in the Gulf of Mexico. There was
room for her to turn, room to run; her bow wave was blue
water with a curl of white foam, and below her keel there
was more blue water down to the hard bottom. Ahead of
her and on all sides there were green islands lying low on
the water, the palms and cedars growing on them out-
lined against the sky, their beaches like white bands between green and blue. To starboard the tip of Pine Island
slipped by, and dead ahead a whirling mass of gulls followed a school of breaking fish, and the screeching and

sound of wings came back to the boat, and the silver fish jumping, the blue water splashing could be easily seen.

"I like this," Nick announced. "Ain't it blue, Ben?"

" 'Isn't' it?" Penny said.

Nick looked at her. "I was talking to the captain of the ship," he said. "Don't you think it's blue, Ben?"

"Mighty blue," Ben said.

"What are the birds doing?"

"Catching fish. Those big fish jumping are after a school of fry—little fish. The sea gulls are getting what's left over."

The whirlwind of gulls suddenly spun up into the air, circled the *Lion's Paw*, and swooped down astern where the fish began to break again.

"I don't see a soul," Penny said. "Doesn't anybody live on these islands?"

"In the winter," Ben said. "There aren't many people on them now, though. And that suits me fine."

"Me too," Nick said. "Which one is Captiva?"

Ben pointed to a lighthouse. "That's the end of Sanibel Island," he said. "It goes along there and laps over Captiva, so you can't see where it begins."

Penny looked at the green islands for a long time. Then in a low voice she said, "We've come a long way, haven't we, Ben? It seems to me that Nick and I ran away a long, long time ago. So long ago that I can hardly remember when we didn't live on this boat."

"I feel that way too," Ben said. "I didn't know that

176

"WE'VE COME A LONG WAY, HAVEN'T WE.
BEN?" PENNY SAID IN A LOW VOICE.

running away took so long. I always thought that you just ran away—bang—and it was all over, but we've been running for more than a week, day and night."

"And now the running away is over," Penny said.

Ben nodded.

"You don't think they'll chase us here?" Nick asked.

Ben shook his head. "I don't think so," he said quietly. "This is cut off from Florida entirely; it's a long way from where we started, and maybe that truck driver mailed that letter in Miami. The way I look at it, when you're looking for something that's moving, each hour that passes makes the area you have to search bigger and bigger. When we first left, Uncle Pete only had to search an area of six miles deep the first hour because that's about as far as we can go in an hour. In two hours he's got twelve miles to hunt around in. We've been gone a lot of hours now—he's got a circle to search from Key West to Savannah. That's a lot of water. And there's no reason for him to suspect that we came through the canal. I think," Ben added slowly, "that it's all over—we've escaped."

"I hope so," Penny said. "Now that we're here I feel free. I had a sort of weight resting on me until now."

Ben grinned. "Oh, brother!" he said. "Weight? It was making an old man out of me. . . . Nick, please go below and get that box of face masks. And in the first-aid kit there's some adhesive tape. Bring that and we'll fix the masks so they'll be watertight."

Nick jumped up, yelling, and, grabbing the coaming of the companionway, swung all the way down without touching the ladder.

"Nick's getting to be quite a sailor," Ben said.

Penny chuckled. "You know, this is doing him a lot of good. You notice how happy he is all the time?"

"How could I help it?" Ben asked.

"Well, back in the orphanage he wasn't ever happy. He just moped around all the time and thought about how to get out."

"An orphanage is no place for a guy like Nick," Ben said. "Or for you either, Penny."

"No," Penny said. Then she said slowly, "Ben, do you think Nick is getting too sassy?"

Ben looked at her and then grinned. "Little boys are naturally sassy. We'll just have to endure it."

"I really don't mind," Penny said. "I like it. He never was sassy in the eganahpro and he's a lot better now."

"He's all right. And if I have anything to do with it, he'll never get put back in that place again. Or you either, Penny."

"We've been away from it too long now," Penny said. "I don't think we could stand it if we got put back in now. I think Nick would just shrivel up and die or something."

Ben looped his leg over the tiller and then stretched his arms out as far as they would go. "Man," he said, "I feel good. There's only one thing that could make me feel better."

Penny looked at him. "Do you think it'll be soon?" she asked.

Ben drew in a deep breath and let it out slowly. "Penny, the other night when we were coming down the canal I had a funny thought. I was thinking about Dad and wondering if he was really dead, and all of a sudden I had this thought. Dad'll come back when we find a Lion's Paw. I don't know why, but I just *know* that."

"I do too," Penny said quietly.

Nick came roaring up out of the hatch. "Which one is going to be mine?" he asked, holding out the box of face masks.

"The one that fits the best," Ben said. "The one with the adhesive on it is the one I've already padded to fit my face. You and Penny try on the other two. Put 'em on and then blow air out of your nose. If the mask doesn't fit you can feel where the air goes out, sort of cool."

As Penny slid the rubber band of the mask over her head she said, "I wonder when my hair will grow out again."

"Never," Nick said.

"You keep quiet," Penny told him.

"Are we going to look for Lions' Paws today, Ben?" Nick asked.

"This afternoon."

"Mine leaks all around," Nick said.

THE LION'S PAW

"Tape it up," Ben directed. He handed Nick his pocket knife. "Just cut off short strips and work them on tight with your fingers."

"Will you teach me how to swim, Ben?" Nick asked.

"Nothing to it," Ben said. "Just put the tip of your tongue against your top teeth so you won't breathe in any water and then wiggle."

"I can do that," Nick declared. He put his tongue against his top teeth and breathed, making a wet, fluttering noise.

"That's the idea."

"Theathy," Nick said.

They were close to the island now and could see the few houses set back among the palm trees. The windows were boarded over with gray planks, and the places looked as though they had been deserted for a long time. With Penny in the bow watching for shallow spots and Nick standing by with the anchor, Ben steered a winding way into a semicircular little bay with tall palm trees growing all around it. The water was glass-smooth, and the white beach seemed to melt into it.

"Let go the anchor," Ben ordered, and Nick rolled the anchor over the side and let the chain rattle out. Ben went forward and looked down into the rising mass of bubbles. The ship rode ahead a few feet, then the chain weight began to snub her and she drifted stern first back past the anchor. Down through the clear water Ben watched the anchor lazily roll over and the two flukes dig down into the firm sand.

182

After they had furled the sails and put on the covers, flemished down the lines and put baggy wrinkle on the anchor chain, put a becket on the tiller to keep the rudder from swinging, secured the chart locker, shut the binnacle, hoisted the owner's pennant, and put the dinghy over the side, Ben stood looking at the near shore. "The end of the voyage," he said quietly. "I don't know which I like best, putting out to sea or coming back after a long time. But whichever it is, after a while I want to do the other."

"I want to go swimming," Nick said.

"Hop in," Ben said.

Nick stared at him. "From here?"

"Why not?" Ben asked. He walked over to the rail and dived in with his pants still on. Nick ran over to the rail and watched Ben's body, sheathed in bubbles, sliding along under the water.

Then Nick leaped.

Penny said, "Nick! For heaven's sake," and rushed to the rail just as Nick, with a curious look on his face, landed feet first in the water and disappeared in the splash he made. In a few seconds Penny could see him down under the water, still sinking, his sun-bleached hair waving slowly around. She began to wring her hands and search around for something to get him out with when Nick's head appeared above the water and he began to thrash around.

Ben came swimming back and treaded water near him.

183

For a little while Nick was so violent in his efforts that he covered himself with foam, but after a few seconds he slowed down.

He had a wild look as he snapped his head around from side to side, looking for something to grab.

"Take it easy," Ben said.

Nick saw the dinghy secured aft and began to flail around again, but this made his head go under and he stopped, coming up to spit and cough.

"Quit moving and hold your head back," Ben said.

Slowly, as Nick held his head as far back as he could, his legs floated upward through the water, his arms floated out, and he was resting peacefully. Penny, looking down into his face, saw the fear go away, a look of amazement take its place in his wild eyes. Then he looked up at her and his face slowly broke into a grin.

"See?" Nick said. "Nothing to it."

"Now just waggle your hands back and forth. Not hard," Ben said.

Nick paddled his hands and began to move slowly through the water. He bumped head on into the side of the sloop, and it surprised him so that he sat up in the water and immediately sank. But he came up without fighting and floated on his back some more.

"Now turn over, shut your mouth, and paddle," Ben said. "When you have to breathe, just lift your head up and breathe slowly through your mouth with your tongue against your teeth."

184

THE LION'S PAW

Nick flopped over in the water, fought it for a few seconds, then relaxed. He paddled along, his face underwater, then raised his head as high as he could and gulped, then paddled some more.

Penny watched him for a long time. She began to get envious as Nick maneuvered around, blowing and gulping like a whale but not drowning.

Suddenly Penny jumped overboard too. She was determined not to make the mistakes Nick had made, but as the water closed over her head with a soft, mushy-sounding sloosh she began instantly to fight. When she thought her head was above water she gasped for breath and sucked in a mouthful of water and foam which choked her and exploded up into her nose. Unable even to breathe, she began to fling her arms around and so went down under the water again.

Suddenly something grabbed her from behind and yanked her up. Ben's voice behind her said quietly, "For crying out loud, what's the rush? Take it easy. You don't have to go anywhere. Now, breathe."

Penny found that she could breathe again, and she lay quietly half upright in the water, Ben holding her up by the collar of her shirt. She didn't want Ben to turn her loose, but when Nick came swimming along toward her and raised his dripping face and looked at her Penny said, "Turn me loose, Ben."

It took all her will power to keep from fighting again, but she didn't, and soon she was paddling around like

185

Nick, raising her head at intervals to breathe, then squeezing her eyes shut and paddling some more. She bumped into Ben, Nick bumped into her, and both of them bumped into the *Lion's Paw*.

Ben said, "If you people would open your eyes and look where you're going you wouldn't damage things so much."

Nick said between pants, "But—it—stings."

"You'll get used to it." Ben threw himself upward and grabbed the gunwale, hauling himself back up onto the boat. He looked down at Penny and Nick slowly and erratically wandering around in the water and grinned to himself as he went below forward and changed into shorts. As he began cooking lunch he heard Penny and Nick breathing like porpoises as they swam around.

After lunch Ben hauled up a full bucket of water and set it abaft the cockpit. "Now, watch," he said.

He got down on his hands and knees and pushed his face down into the bucket. In a few seconds he blew air out through his nose, turned his mouth up clear of the water, breathed in, then turned his face back into the bucket. He did that two or three times, then stood up, wiping his face. "Do it that way," he said.

Nick tried it first and swallowed a good deal of water before he learned how. When he finally stood up he patted his stomach with both hands. "Listen," he said. "Hear it? I'm full of water."

"Good for you," Ben said.

THE LION'S PAW

After they had both learned to breathe properly they went back to fixing the face masks with the tape. When they were fixed they tested them in the bucket of water and learned all over again how to breathe, because if they blew out through their noses with the mask on it pushed the mask loose and water flooded in.

Ben found one of his old bathing suits for Penny, and she cut off the legs of the new overalls to make a bathing suit for Nick. With the face masks and each one carrying a sock, they climbed down into the dinghy and Ben rowed them ashore.

"It'd be funny if we just walked out and picked up a Lion's Paw first thing," Nick said.

"Don't worry," Ben said.

They walked, wearing tennis shoes, through the stiff, head-high grass and under the coconut trees where land crabs made a rattling noise going down into their holes. At the edge of a marshy place dozens of white herons rose out of a tree and flew over them, their long legs tucked up and streaming out behind.

And then they reached the seaward beach. Nick and Penny stopped in their tracks. Almost whispering, Penny said, "Millions!"

"Billions!" Nick said.

Even Ben had never seen anything like it. Sea shells of a thousand kinds covered the beach. Where a storm had hit there were dunes and cliffs of nothing but sea shells. As Nick had said, there were billions of them.

187

THE LION'S PAW

Penny's voice was stricken. "How can we find one shell in all these?"

Ben stood looking down the long, curving, empty beach. "I—don't—know," he said. Inside he felt defeated. There were too many shells, too many millions of them. As the gentle waves rolled in from the endless expanse of the Gulf they washed more shells, rolling and tinkling, up on the littered beach.

"I'm ready," Nick said. "What does a Lion's Paw look like?"

Ben turned slowly and looked at him. Nothing seemed to defeat Nick, Ben thought.

Ben went along the beach for a little way until he found an orange-colored pecten—a round, slightly curved shell forming half of a whole bivalve. On the outside there were straight, smooth furrows, almost like those of a plowed field, which radiated from the hinge to the fluted outer edge. "A Lion's Paw looks like this," Ben said. "Only there aren't but nine or ten of these furrows and they aren't so smooth and even. They have knobs on them like the joints of your fingers, and on the ends they have a bigger knob—like the toenail of a lion."

Nick studied the pecten for a moment, then put on his face mask. "I'll go get one," he said, and waded down into the water, stooped over until his mask went down into it, and then pushed away with his feet and began to paddle slowly along, looking down at the more millions of shells lying on the bottom of the Gulf.

188

Penny and Ben slowly joined him.

The search for the Lion's Paw had begun along the miles of deserted beach. Almost invisible as they lay face down in the water, their heads showing a little as they turned up to breathe, their bodies being gently washed and rolled by the waves, they searched the bottom with their eyes, turned over shells one by one with their reaching hands.

When their fingers were wrinkled and stiff like an old man's neck and their bodies were waterlogged and their faces creased in a circle by the pressure of the masks, they ended the first day's hunt for the Lion's Paw.

"I've got some beauties," Nick said as they walked back across the island. He held up the wet, bulging sock. "And I almost caught a fish with my bare hands. He was funny-looking, Ben. He would go along the bottom, and every now and then two long whiskers would poke out under his chin and he'd wave them around in the sand. I almost caught him."

"Goatfish," Ben said. "They dig up food with those whiskers."

"Could you catch one?"

"Might," Ben said.

As they crossed the road a black snake six feet long slithered like lightning into the bushes and disappeared. Penny and Nick backed up, but Ben said, "Won't hurt you," and went on in the same direction the snake had gone. "He's probably five miles from here by now."

189

THE LION'S PAW

"He went faster than that alligator," Nick declared.

"But watch out for a little snake with a blunt nose and a sort of blunt tail. That's a coral snake," Ben said. "It has yellow, pink, and gray bands with black lines separating them and it's very dangerous. If you see one stay away from it."

"Don't worry," Penny said. "I don't like snakes."

"There was an eganap who had a snake one time," Nick said, "but they wouldn't let him keep it. It was a little green snake."

"Dad knows a lot about snakes," Ben said. "He explained to me how the poison works, but I've sort of forgotten. Some snakes poison you with some stuff that works on your blood—sort of like blood poisoning, I guess. But other snakes, like the coral snake, give you a poison that paralyzes your nerves so that whatever makes your heart beat can't work any more, so you die."

Penny shivered. "I don't like 'em."

"I like 'em better'n Uncle Pete," Nick said. "At least they don't chase you."

"He's not all that bad," Ben said. "He's just a nuisance. He'd make a good old maid."

Nick laughed. "Penny, you remember Old Mrs. Martin at the orphanage? She should have been a man. She had whiskers and a voice like a bullfrog."

When they got back aboard the sloop Nick poured his sockful of shells into a cardboard box. Penny and Ben hadn't picked up any.

190

"BUT WATCH OUT FOR A LITTLE SNAKE WITH
A BLUNT NOSE AND A SORT OF BLUNT TAIL,"
BEN SAID.

Ben looked at Nick's shells and told him the names of some of them.

"I'm going to be like your dad," Nick said. "I'm going to have a collection of sea shells and when I go all around the world I'll get some everywhere I go."

"We aren't doing this right," Ben said. "No system. Tomorrow I think two of us ought to swim and one walk on the beach. We'll take turns. That way we'll cover more ground. And we won't stay in the water so long. Three or four hours is plenty to stay in the water, I think."

"I do too," Penny said. "I feel a little bit funny— from swallowing so much water, I guess."

"Well, then, that's the way we'll do it tomorrow."

"It didn't make me feel funny," Nick said. "Just hungry."

"If you and Penny will cook, I'll fix the engine," Ben said. "It needs new intake connections and a lot of things, and it looks like we'll be here plenty long enough to do them all."

"Penny'll cook and I'll help you," Nick said.

"There isn't room for but one man in the engine room," Ben said. "You help Penny."

"Oh, all right," Nick said. "Come on, Penny, you galley slave."

Chapter 13

HE search for the Lion's Paw went on day after day. The brassy sun hammered down on them, burning their knees and forearms and the backs of their necks to a deep mahogany, peeling their noses and foreheads and the backs of their knees. Nick's collection of shells piled higher and higher in the cardboard box, but they found no Lions' Paws—not even a broken piece of one.

Each morning after they had had breakfast and then made everything shipshape below and topside they would row ashore in the dinghy, secure it to a palm tree, and walk across to the seaward beach. As two of them swam along, one would search the piles of shells on the sand. Then the one on land would put on his face mask and one of the others would come out on land. Steadily, for hundreds of yards each day, they worked their way down the long, curving, and deserted beach of Captiva Island. In the late afternoon they would stop, put up a marker to show where to start in the morning, and go back to the sloop. While Penny and Nick cooked supper Ben worked on the engine. When he got the intake water line off he found a lot of corrosion in the jacket, so he took that off. When he got that off he found a lot of carbon in the head, so he tackled that. After four days he almost had the engine taken apart.

Each one of them gradually felt the feeling of defeat growing. They each kept their feelings secret from one another, but as the days went by and they didn't find the shell they began to give up hope.

One morning when they got to the beach they found the Gulf so muddy that, even in shallow water, they couldn't see the bottom through the face masks.

"Must be a storm out there somewhere," Ben said. "I hope it doesn't hit us."

"What would it do to us?" Nick asked.

"The boat's sheltered all right, so it wouldn't do any damage," Ben said. "We'd just lose a day or so unless we wanted to hunt in a pouring rain and a yowling wind."

"You mean we'd just have to stay on the boat all day?" Nick asked.

Ben nodded.

"I wouldn't mind," Nick said. "I'm getting a little tired of hunting all day long every day."

THE LION'S PAW

It was the first time anyone had said what each one was thinking. They were all getting tired. Ben looked at Nick and then at Penny. Ben didn't want to give up; the thought of it scared him, but he knew that Penny and Nick were discouraged and that if they didn't find one soon it would be bad. Ben remembered the night coming down the canal. His father would come back when they found a Lion's Paw. The belief in that was still strong; in fact, it had grown stronger as each day passed.

"Maybe a rest would do us all good," Ben said. "In a few days we'll have to go for provisions anyway, so we'll take the day off, sail up to Boca Grande or someplace, get some food and fresh water, then sail back. We'll fish."

"Oh, boy," Nick said. "When?"

"What's the food situation, Penny?" Ben asked.

"Good," she said. "We won't need anything for at least two days."

"All right. We'll hunt for two more days, then take a day off," Ben said.

"I'll be able to see better," Nick said. "I'll just rest my eyes all that day, and then when we start again they'll be much brighter."

All three of them searched the beach that day. By afternoon the wind was blowing strong out of the northwest and the muddy waves were breaking and foaming far up the beach. They rolled a lot of horseshoe crabs up on their backs and Nick began collecting them, but they

196

ALL THREE OF THEM SEARCHED THE BEACH
THAT DAY.

were heavy, so he dropped them after a while and just collected shells.

On the way back to the boat Ben said, "This weather doesn't look very good—for shelling or fishing."

"That's all right," Nick said. "If we can't go anywhere I can spread out my collection and see what I've got."

"You know," Penny said as she walked along, "I haven't thought about running away and all that for a long time."

"Neither have I," Ben said. "I guess Uncle Pete has given up by now, don't you?"

"How long has it been?" Penny asked.

Ben laughed. "I haven't got the faintest idea. Seems like years since we shoved off that night."

"It certainly does. Anyway," Penny said, "I don't think anyone is looking for us any more. Everybody's forgotten about us."

"We'll turn on the radio tonight and see if they still talk about us," Ben said. "But not for long, because it'll run down the batteries and I haven't got the engine fixed yet."

"How much have you got to do?"

"If we have to stay aboard tomorrow I'll finish it," Ben said. "I don't want to go up to Boca Grande with it out of commission."

"Look at all the sea gulls," Nick said. "I never saw so many."

Ben shook his head. "We're going to have some real

weather," he said. "Those are ocean-going gulls over there. When they come in to shore it means the weather is really stinking."

"What would happen to them if they stayed out?" Nick asked.

"I don't know," Ben said. "Dad and I were out in a real howler one time. The wind was blowing woofty miles an hour—blowing so hard it held the waves down and just smoked 'em, blowing the foam off so that everything looked gray. I saw some gulls then; they were just sitting on the water, going up and down with the waves. Didn't seem to bother 'em much. But I've always noticed that when the weather's making up most gulls come in to shore."

Then, as they came out on the narrow shell road, they saw the man. They were surprised to see him because it was the first person they had seen since they had been on the island, but none of them thought of him as being dangerous, as being a threat. They had forgotten how it felt to be always hunted.

The man was very tall and skinny as a rail, with long bony arms and a thin chest under his overall straps. He was so thin they could see all his ribs. He had a fish net folded over his shoulder, the cork floats and lead weights flapping. Ben nodded and they all said, "Good evening," and started to walk on across the road.

The man moved a little and blocked their way.

"Wait a minute," he said. He had an unpleasant voice.

200

His face was as long and thin as the rest of him, and his nose was so thin Nick wondered how he could breathe through it. His little eyes were set close to the nose so that his face looked like some sort of bird's face. His eyes were hard and glittery like a bird's.

"What you kids doin' aroun' here?" the man asked.

"Just looking for sea shells," Ben said.

"Where you come from?"

"Fort Myers," Ben said.

"Come on the ferry?"

Ben shook his head. "We came over in a boat."

"Whose boat?"

Ben felt his anger packing up inside him. "Mr. Jenkins's," he said.

"Never heard of no Jenkins aroun' here. I think you're lying."

"What for?" Ben asked. "Can't people come here and look for sea shells?"

The man shifted the fish net on his shoulder. "I don't see that you've got any shells," he said.

Nick held up his sockful of shells and shook it up and down. "You can't see very well," Nick said.

The man stooped down so that his face was on a level with Nick's. "You keep your trap shut, bub," he said.

Ben stepped over beside Nick. "Come on. Let's go," he said.

As Ben started to walk across the road the man put his hand on Ben's chest and shoved him backward a step or two. "Now, just hold on," the man said. "When I say you can go you can go. Understand?"

Ben put his hands in his pockets and doubled up his fists.

The man pointed a bony finger almost into Penny's eye. "What's your name?" he demanded.

Penny's mouth opened, but Ben said first, "Her name's Anne. Anne Jackson."

The man glared at Ben. "Who asked you?"

Ben went on, "His is Bill Jackson, and mine's Charlie Jackson."

The man spat a stream of yellow juice out of his mouth, and it dribbled a little down the corner and into the stubble of his whiskers. He began to rock back and forth on his heels. "I think your name is Sturges," he said. "And I think these two brats is orphans."

Ben felt something cold grip his heart. He shook his head slowly. "Our name is Jackson," he said.

Around a bend in the road a ramshackle Ford truck rattled up to them. A man stuck his head out and looked at them.

"What's goin' on?" the driver asked.

"I think these kids is them runaways from the east coast," the thin man said. "But they say their name is Jackson."

"Maybe it is. How would they git here from the east coast?" the driver asked. "Come on, git in or we'll miss the ferry."

202

The man threw the net in the back of the truck and started to get in. "If these is them runaways, Joe," he said, "you're just costing me five hundred dollars."

"Git in! Git in!" the driver said. "Ferry's leaving in five minutes."

The thin man got in, and as the truck drove away they saw him lean out and look back at them.

They stood silently in the road for a few moments, and at last Ben said, "I guess we were wrong."

Penny nodded. "They're still chasing us," she said.

"What was that he spat out of his mouth?" Nick asked.

"Tobacco juice," Ben said. "Come on."

"Are we going to have to go?" Penny asked.

"I don't know," Ben said. "But we've got to be more careful. Tonight we'll pull the sloop in closer to the trees."

"If we have to go, is there any other place where we can find a Lion's Paw?" Penny asked.

"I don't think so. I never heard of any," Ben said.

"The next man we see like that," Nick said, "we'll jump on him. Ben, you get him on top, and Penny'll get his middle, and I'll get his feet. I'll bite his leg off."

"Boy," Ben said, "I felt like hitting that thin drink of water when he called me a liar." Ben swung his fist in a short arc. Then in a low voice he said, "I wish my dad had heard that. He would have hit him just once. Just—one—time."

They rowed in silence out to the sloop, and Ben immediately went below and brought up a long telescope. Resting it on the gallows frame, he began scanning the far end of the island.

"There's the ferry," he said. "Heading for Punta Rassa. The truck's on it."

Penny sighed. "At least he won't bother us tonight."

Ben shut the telescope and put it back into its leather case. "I don't think he'll bother us any more," he said slowly. "He probably won't even come back here again. They didn't have any fish, did they?"

"I don't think so," Penny said. "There wasn't anything but a net in the back of the truck."

"If they don't catch fish over here, what's the use of coming back?" Ben asked. "We'll be more careful, but I don't think we'll have to worry about that bean pole any more."

"Didn't he look like a bird?" Nick asked.

"Mean-looking," Penny said.

Ben went down and tapped the barometer. The needle jumped downward. "We've got about one more day for the beach," Ben said, "then it'll be blowing so hard the birds will be walking."

In the morning, before they rowed ashore, Ben locked all the hatches securely, battened down the topside, and turned the cushions up in the cockpit in case of rain. It was an ugly gray morning, with the wind blowing half a gale out of the northwest. Old fronds from the coconut trees thrashed around and were torn off; the tall grass was lying half flat. On the beach the sea was coming in in great brown rollers so that the whole length of the beach was shrouded in a smoke of foam, and there was a steady thunderous booming.

"This is what tears the shells loose and brings 'em ashore," Ben said as they started the slow, head-down, stooped-over walking in search of a Lion's Paw.

Nick had his old sock and was, by choice, walking the beach nearest the sea. Penny had the middle strip and Ben the inland edge. It was hardest for Nick because he was continually being threatened by the breakers.

By the time they stopped to eat lunch the weather was foul, the sky hanging down gray just above them, the wind so strong they almost had to yell to talk. They were all soaked to the skin from the flying spray, and the wind was cold.

But they went on. Something was driving Ben, some knowledge he had that he couldn't understand or express. He just knew that they had to keep on searching until the last minute.

They found nothing. Of the millions of new shells washed up by the storm, no Lions' Paws were recognized.

Nick's sock was overflowing when they finally gave up and left the beach. They didn't talk much as they walked across the island, for they were discouraged and depressed.

By the time they got to the bay where the sloop was it was almost dark. Ben rowed the dinghy in silence and they climbed out, one by one, and lifted the dinghy up and turned it upside down over the cabin skylight.

Penny went aft to get the lashings for it, and as she stepped down into the cockpit a voice said, "Howdy."

It paralyzed Penny for a second and then she screamed, "Ben!"

The thin man got slowly up from where he had been sitting in the cockpit. Ben and Nick came running aft, then stopped short as they saw him.

The sloop swung a few degrees and showed the man's boat tied up astern.

"Just the way I figgered it," the man said. "You painted her black, didn't you? And changed the name?"

"I don't know what you're talking about," Ben said. "And you'd better get off this boat."

The man took a step toward Ben. "Do you want to get some teeth smacked out?"

Ben didn't move. "My father will be here soon," he said.

"Yeah? Listen," the man said, coming closer to Ben, "I know all about your father. He's dead. I know all about you too, bub. Your name ain't no more Jackson than mine is."

Nick gripped his sockful of sea shells and advanced toward the man. Ben held him back with an arm across his chest.

"You've made a mistake," Ben said to the man quietly. "Now, please get off this boat."

206

THE LION'S PAW

"Mind your talk!" the man snapped. "I'll git off when I'm plumb good and ready. Any more back talk from you and I'll smack you down, understand?"

Ben felt desperate—and helpless. His voice broke a little as he said, "My father will throw you off this boat when he gets here."

"Your father ain't throwin' nothin' nowhere 'cause he's dead as a mackerel. Now, you listen. I done got the number of this boat off the carlin' and I'm goin' across the bay and check it—just to be sure this here boat's the *Hard A Lee* like I think it is. After I do that I'll telegraph that feller on the east coast. Then I'm comin' back here and stay until he gits here and gives me the reward. No use your tryin' to sneak out of here because if you sail out tonight you'll git on a reef and end up drownded. And don't try hidin'. There's no place on this little island where I can't find you. Understand?" The man hitched up his overalls and stepped out of the cockpit.

"Lion's Paw," he said, his voice sneering.

He climbed down into his boat, started the engine, and chugged out of the little bay. They stood in the cockpit and watched as his boat began slapping into the little waves of the sheltered harbor.

In their silence they listened to the wind now whining through the rigging, listened to the dry roaring sound it made in the palm fronds and over the grass, listened to the constant far booming of the surf against the seaward side of the island.

"I was wrong," Ben said quietly. "He came back."

Penny nodded.

"Can't we get away?" Nick asked.

"We've got to try," Ben said. "But I'm scared. The only thing we can do is try to beat our way out through the Pass, then get off this lee shore as far as we can and heave to."

"Couldn't we go to another island and hide?" Penny asked.

Ben shook his head. "Not in this storm at night. We'd hit a reef, and in five minutes this boat would be nothing but splinters. We'd drown."

"But can he get back through the storm?" Penny asked.

"Those fishing boats can live through anything. His boat doesn't draw more than a few inches of water—goes right over reefs that we'd pile up on. He'll be back—tonight."

"And the engine isn't fixed either," Nick said.

"I know it," Ben said. He looked at Penny and Nick in the gathering darkness. "I want you to know what we're in for," he said quietly. "If we stay here we'll get caught. As soon as he looks up our number in the yacht register he'll know for sure who we are. I'll have to go back to Uncle Pete and let him sell the boat. You'll have to go back to the orphanage. On the other hand, if we try to make the Pass we may hit a reef. If we got through the Pass I think we could get sea room and be all right. . . . What do you want to do? Stay or go? . . . Penny?"

Penny rubbed her finger around and around the glass of her face mask.

"Let's go," Nick said.

Penny nodded.

"All right," Ben said. "We try for the Pass."

"We can make it all right," Nick said. "We're good sailors now."

"I hope so," Ben said. "I hate to have a dumb plow jockey like that mess us up. If that guy had any sense he would have made us go with him—at least one of us. It burns me up to get caught by that stupid string bean."

"I don't guess we'll ever find a Lion's Paw now," Penny said.

"Nope. . . . Well, let's get on the ball. Nick, please go below and bring up that storm jib in the sail locker. It's got a tag on it with red letters, 'Storm Jib.' "

"Aye, aye," Nick said. On his way through the main cabin he emptied his sockful of shells into the box with the others.

Topside, while Ben got the sails ready, Penny and Nick closed and battened all the hatches, put a cap on the Charlie Noble, and took all loose gear below. The dinghy was upside down on the main cabin skylight.

It was dark when they got sail on her and weighed anchor.

Chapter 14

HE *Lion's Paw* sailed with deceptive smoothness out of the shelter of the little bay. Ben had rolled a triple reef in her mainsail and had rigged a small storm jib, but even under this canvas the wind was so strong that she lifted and churned out a white foaming wake. The three of them huddled in the cockpit, Ben steering, the wind abeam as they made easting out toward deeper water. The chart showed treacherous reefs and shallow water scattered all over Pine Island Sound, and Ben had to pick a winding course through them until he could get high enough to give him a straight shot through Captiva Pass and into the open Gulf.

As soon as the sloop left the shelter of the bay she began to pound along through the choppy, vicious, shallow-water waves. The wind heeled her over even under the shortened sail, and spray curling over the windward scupper lashed back into the cockpit. Ben squinted his eyes against it and took crude bearings on the red-and-green flashing buoys he could see dimly through the haze of spray and which marked the channel up the Sound. As the buoys seemed to move farther and farther away it meant that the boat was getting into more dangerous water. Ben hated to hold her and drive her into it, but he had to take her almost into the shallows in order to get a clear shot, off the wind, at the Pass.

The feeling of danger was everywhere and held them silent as the minutes dragged out. Whenever the boat was lifted by a wave Ben unconsciously tried to hold her up with the muscles of his body, and when she slammed down his stomach would turn cold.

It was pitch dark now, and all they could see was the grayness of the water streaked with lines of darkness where the wind whipped across it. Ben, clinging to the tiller with one hand, to the binnacle with the other, and bracing his legs against the side of the cockpit, took sights on two buoys across the top of the compass and knew from their angle that he was far up into the shallows. At each plunge of the boat he waited for the dreadful crush and halting stagger a boat makes when it strikes bottom under sail and a driving wind. If she should strike now Ben knew that it would be the end of her, for the wind and waves would instantly conquer her and drive her on against the reef, and the jagged reef would claw out her bottom and let the sea crush her oak ribs.

But he held her minute after minute, for he knew that if he turned too soon the leeway under shortened sail would put her down below the Pass and they would have it to do all over again. Through the cold of the wind and the spray he felt sweat breaking, and his hand on the tiller began to tremble. Peering at the gray, streaked water, he imagined that a reef lay hidden under every foot of it.

At last the buoy was far astern, its light almost invisible in the driving spray .

"Ready about," Ben shouted.

Penny and Nick stood by the sheets.

"Don't let her get away from you," Ben yelled. "She mustn't go backward an inch or she'll go aground. Stand by!"

Penny and Nick braced their feet.

"Helm alee!" Ben shouted.

The bow of the *Lion's Paw* staggered up into the wind, hung for what seemed a minute of pure agony as the stiff storm canvas flapped with a sound like rifles and the wind and sea seemed to leap on her, trying to drive her backward into the reefs, then she came through.

"Clamp her!" Ben yelled, and Penny and Nick slammed turns around the bitts, the wet rope hard and rough in their hands.

The jib filled with a sharp slap, and Ben felt life come

212

THE LION'S PAW

back into the boat. The mainsail luffed viciously, then also
filled, and Ben sighed and slumped a little at the tiller.

"Well done," he said as Penny and Nick came back to
sit beside him. "So far so good."

"Fine," Nick said. "I like this."

Ben could only grunt.

"It's sort of wild," Nick said.

"Bro-ther!" Ben said.

"Where are we now?" Penny asked.

"We're leaving the reefs. The Pass is a little down to
port. We ought to hit it right in the eye." Relief was
sweeping over Ben, and he began to feel confident that
they could get through the Pass. Once through that,
which he knew would be rugged, they would be almost
free.

"How can you tell when you get there?" Penny asked.

Ben almost laughed. "Don't worry, Penny, you'll know
it when we get there. This wind is trying to shove the
whole Gulf of Mexico through that Pass. This is like sailing on a frog pond compared to what that will be."

Penny moved a little closer to Ben. "Are you scared,
Ben?"

"Sure," Ben said. "And I'll be scared until we get her
hove to. This isn't fun, Penny."

"I didn't think so," Penny said. "But I like it. Could
the boat turn over, Ben?"

"No. But she'll come so close to it, it won't make much
difference. Are the hatches all closed and battened?"

"Yes," Penny said. "We put the bars on all of them."

"Good. In a few minutes we're going to be under the water a lot more than we're going to be on top of it."

"I better get my face mask," Nick said.

"No, just hang on." Ben reached behind him and got the flemished towline. "Here," he said, pushing it at Nick, "you and Penny tie this around yourselves, so if you're washed overboard you can get back on again."

"Is it going to be that bad?" Penny asked, her voice small.

"Worse," Ben said, tying the becket around his own waist.

With the wind almost abeam and steaming down on her, the *Lion's Paw* rocketed toward the open mouth of the Pass. Sheets of spray broke over the scuppers and exploded back into the cockpit; her rolling and pitching kept yanking at the sheets, and the crack of waves beating against her forefoot sounded like artillery fire.

Then the *Lion's Paw* struck the waters of the narrow Pass. With the wind flailing across the open Gulf, waves were being piled up in the Pass until they were higher than the palm trees on the islands bordering it. The whine of wind and the sound of waves changed to a deep, steady roaring which seemed to speak of the power of the charging water.

The *Lion's Paw* caught the first huge wave right in the teeth, and it stood her up on her stern so that Penny and Nick had to claw to keep from being thrown out of the

214

THE "LION'S PAW" CAUGHT THE FIRST HUGE
WAVE RIGHT IN THE TEETH.

cockpit. Then, as the wave roared out from under her, she seemed to hang for a second in the air before she fell back with a splash which sent a spurting white blanket of foam from all around her.

"Wow!" Nick yelled, and grabbed for the coaming again as a wave jolted the stern up and the sloop pitched straight down into the trough of the next one. She was down in the trough, walloping as though wounded, when the wave hit her. The curling top of it—it looked to Ben like a black wall with a white top of foam—crashed down on the foredeck, rushed aft and crushed into the cockpit, smashing all three of them back against the coaming and knocking the wind out of them.

Blinded by the water and gasping for breath, Ben held her only by the feel of the ship in his body, the tug and lurch of the tiller in his hand.

Then Ben became conscious of the pounding somewhere forward. As soon as he heard it clearly he knew that he had been hearing it for a long time. He straightened, the spray beating straight into his face, and listened.

"Penny," he yelled. "There's something adrift. Do you think you could get below without being washed overboard?"

"I'll try," Penny said.

Another wave came galloping aboard, smothered them in swirling water, and when it was gone Ben heard the pounding again, loud now and ominous.

"Hang on with both hands," he yelled, as Penny, the

217

rope around her waist untied, staggered up the cockpit and wrenched at the companion hatch. She disappeared through it, closing the doors, as a wave stood the boat on her bow.

The noise of the pounding worried Ben, but as the boat fought her way forward and wasn't killed by the waves crashing down on her, he began to think that they would get through the Pass. In a moment's lull he listened and could not hear the pounding.

"Maybe Penny found whatever it was and lashed it down," Ben thought.

A wave lifted the *Lion's Paw* to the very top of its crest, and before she slithered down again Ben shielded his eyes and tried to see ahead. He wasn't sure, but he thought that, three waves ahead, the sea began to look calmer. That would be the end of the Pass.

"Stand by!" Ben yelled to Nick as he watched the next one coming. It was a brute, and Ben crouched, his head down in his shoulders, as the wave zizzled toward them, towered above the boat as though suddenly frozen, then curled slowly and smoothly and fell down. Tons of water struck the deck and came aft. When the wall of it hit the mast the wave was sliced open, white water exploding up the mast.

Then at last Ben knew what had been making the pounding noise.

Part of the wave on deck sluiced under the dinghy, lifted it up, whirled it half around. Then more water

218

smashed it down, bow first. The dinghy crashed through the main cabin skylight, almost slipped through into the cabin, but the water jerked it out again, rolled it keel over gunwale across the panes of glass, ground it over the varnished top of the companion hatch, and dumped it on its side into the cockpit.

Ben, still hearing the distinct tinkling the breaking glass had made, knew that disaster had struck them. With the main cabin roof sliced half open, there was nothing to stop the water from pouring into the boat. And, like a tiny break in a dam, this wound in the *Lion's Paw* would be ripped and smashed ever wider.

But they were almost through the Pass. Ben remembered how the water had looked calmer only three waves away. If they could make it to the Gulf he could turn her down into easier water; he could keep the waves off the deck. He could get her out to sea.

Ben clamped his jaws tight and began to nurse his stricken ship. With all the skill he had he eased her toward the next wave, tried to lift her into it, tried to let her run off so that the wave wouldn't break on the deck.

He failed and knew it as he and Nick were smothered with rushing water.

As the deck cleared, the scuppers spouting white fans of water, the companion hatch opened and Penny's face, a gray blur in the darkness, appeared.

"Ben, *Ben,*" she yelled. "The cabin's full of water. Ben!"

"Okay," Ben said.

Almost crying inside, the defeat like a wet weight on his heart, Ben shoved the tiller to leeward, the bow swung up into the wind, and the boat turned on her heel and began to run back through the Pass, wounded, heavy with water, wallowing before the seas now, back into the Sound. There was no more fighting and clawing and smashing now, only the smooth running, the whining wind above them—soon the almost gentle slap-slap of waves as they sailed back into the shelter of the islands.

Penny came back into the cockpit. "What happened?" she asked.

Ben's voice was empty as he said, "I forgot to secure the dinghy. . . . When that man was aboard. . . . I forgot all about it."

"What are we doing now?" Nick asked. "It's not rough any more."

They could hardly hear Ben as he said, "We're—going back."

"To the bay?" Penny asked slowly.

"To the bay," Ben said. "Got to. She's ripped open, Penny. Another wave on deck would have swamped her."

Penny felt tears in her eyes. "Just a little thing like that," she said slowly. "Just a little rope we didn't tie."

"Yep," Ben said. "We were almost through the Pass. Oh, *blast* it!"

"Maybe that man has come back already and gone away when we weren't there," Nick said hopefully.

"I doubt it. We haven't been gone long enough."

"Well, maybe we can patch up the skylight," Nick said.

"We're really going to try," Ben said. "We'll bail her out as soon as we anchor. Then we'll try to patch the holes. Then if that man hasn't come back we'll try the Pass again. I'm sure we can make it and I think the wind's dying a little."

The *Lion's Paw* crept back into the familiar little bay. They stood up, scanning the dark, calm water, looking for a shadow against the curving white sand of the beach. The bay was empty.

At anchor, the sails down but just looped around the boom and guy, Ben and Nick and Penny went below into the cabin.

The wreckage down there amazed them when Ben turned on the light. With only the gentle waves slowly rocking the boat, the water in the cabin, shining with oil from the engine, flowed back and forth, slapping with little pats at the walls, the table legs, the hatches. The water was almost three feet deep down there, and its little waves broke over into Penny's and Nick's bunks.

Floating in the water was everything that could float. The book shelves were empty. The walls around the cabin had been stripped of everything—Nick's box of shells, Ben's father's boxes, charts, the clock and barometer, food, foul-weather gear—everything. Only the storm lantern hung cockeyed from the overhead. And as they waded into it they felt stuff breaking under their feet—sea shells crunching, broken glass, the tangle of clothes, china. In a corner a sou'wester floated upright, bumping gently against the galley bulkhead. Above them, through the broken and jagged skylight, they could see the dark, lowering sky and hear the whine of wind.

For an instant Ben was utterly defeated by the ugly, oily water, and he stood with it washing around his legs and just looked at it. Then he rallied a little. "If you and Penny will bail, I'll start patching," he said. "Get a bucket. One stay on deck and empty and the other lift the bucket up. Better take turns because the one below does most of the work."

Nick went wading around in the cabin, feeling for a bucket. Ben felt around for the tool chest in the submerged engine room and after he had found it went forward for canvas and wood.

Then the long hours began. Nick took the first trick on deck. Penny, kneeling on the table in the middle of the cabin, dipped the bucket full of the slimy water, then lifted it, sloshing some always over herself, up to Nick reaching down through the broken skylight. Nick would drop the empty bucket down and Penny would grab it before it sank, fill it again, lift it again.

It seemed endless. Penny's back began to ache from lifting; her knees turned raw from kneeling. And the water didn't seem to go down. She kept watching the line the little breaking wavelets made on the bulkhead, and it didn't seem to go down.

Ben, on deck, tore out the broken part of the skylight and then began to build a crude frame where it had been. With the storm lantern for light he worked as fast as he could but still hating each nail he had to drive down into the solid mahogany he had spent so many years varnishing, swabbing, scraping, and sanding. He hated the nails he hammered down into the rock-hard teak of the deck, hated the strokes of the hammer when he missed the nail and slammed a round indentation into the wood.

Nick and Penny changed places, and it was very hard for Nick because he wasn't as tall as Penny.

Slowly, not even by inches, the water went down, leaving a slime of oil on the cabin bulkheads. When Ben's frame was ready they had to change and carry the bucket up the companionway and dump it into the self-bailing cockpit, while Ben spread a heavy storm sail over his frame and nailed it down, using fiddles off the table, holdbacks from the racks, and anything else he could find for strips.

At last the skylight was solid again. Ben came sloshing down into the cabin and looked at the band of oil where the water had been.

"Fine!" he said. "We can get going in a little while."

He went on into his cabin, where he could now reach the bilge pump without drowning. Sitting down in the water and bracing his feet, he began to turn the handle of the pump. He thought as he turned it and felt the water rushing through the valve that he would tell his father never to put a bilge pump so low that it couldn't be used in case of a disaster like this one.

And then, because he knew that they could try the Pass again as soon as the water went down another inch or so, Ben began to work frantically at the pump. Time was running out for them—the wind was dying as the night dragged to an end. Soon the man would be back. Ben kept listening for the chug-chug of the one-cylinder engine.

When there was less than a foot of water remaining in the main cabin Penny took over at the pump. Ben and Nick went topside.

The storm had passed. The sky, as though ashamed of the glooming clouds and the wind, was clearing to windward, so that they could see the band of stars. Above them the moon made a dim patch in the whirling clouds.

"Let's get these reefs out," Ben said, "and the storm jib off. We're going to need all the sail we can handle when we try it again."

"We'll make it this time," Nick said as he helped take the reefs out of the mainsail. "And it won't be so rough, will it?"

"Not quite. There'll still be a heavy sea running in the Pass."

The eastern sky was growing gray when Ben at last said, "Let's go, Nick." His voice was happy again.

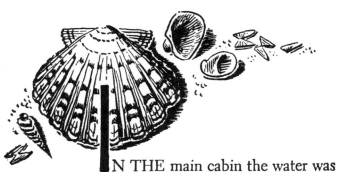

Chapter 15

N THE main cabin the water was now only a few inches deep, and Penny at the bilge pump was pulling it out fast. As Ben began searching through the dirty and soaked charts he called, "How you making, Penny?"

"Fine," Penny called back, her voice a little muffled.

"We're leaving as soon as I can find the chart," Ben said. "No sign of that man yet, and the storm's over."

"I'll keep on pumping," Penny said.

"Is this the one?" Nick asked, holding out a soggy sheet of heavy paper. Ben wiped some of the oil off it with his shirt.

"That's it. Let's go!"

Ben snapped off the cabin light, leaving only the one burning where Penny was, and started for the hatch. Nick

THE LION'S PAW

was right behind him. Their feet splashed in the shallow water.

A sound came down to them, drifting, hardly audible. Ben stopped and stopped Nick with his hand. They stood in the darkness, not breathing, not moving.

The sound came again. It was like something clawing at hard wood. It went on for a few seconds, stopped, and then they heard a dim, muffled splash.

"Get Penny!" Ben ordered.

Nick, trying not to splash, went forward. "Penny," he whispered, "come quick."

Penny came out of the cabin, her clothes dripping water loudly down into the water on the floor.

"The light," Ben's whisper floated back to them.

Penny snapped off the light.

"What's the matter?" she whispered.

"I don't know," Nick said. "We heard a noise."

Together they waded back through the cabin to stand beside Ben.

"Did you hear it again?" Nick asked.

"No." Ben stooped to the toolbox and with both hands feeling he silently got out a Stillson wrench, a big ball-peen hammer, and a heavy-handled screw driver.

"If it's the man," Ben whispered, "he's not going to stop us now—I don't care what we have to do. Penny, you stand over there against the bookcase. Nick, you get under the table. I'll be over here. When he comes in let him have it. Penny, you swing right at his middle. I'll try

226

for his head and, Nick, you whack him across the shins. Keep pasting him until we get him down, then jump him." Then Ben said slowly, "We're leaving here. Nothing's going to stop us this time."

In the cabin there was no sound except their soft breathing. Outside the wind was now blowing gently; the waves against the hull of the boat made a little lip-lapping sound.

Then they heard the scrabbling noise again. Now it was clearer—like fingernails scratching on wood. And there was, this time, no splash when the scratching noise stopped.

They waited, holding their breaths.

On deck something thumped. Thumped again. Water dripped on the wood with a sharp, clear, wet sound. Someone began to walk very slowly toward the cockpit.

Ben gripped the wet, oily handle of the wrench and measured his distance against the doorway into the cabin. The man was very tall—he would have to stoop to come through the door. As he was stooped over Ben would bring the wrench down, Penny would swing the hammer head into his ribs, Nick would lace his shins with the butt of the screw driver.

The footsteps on deck were soft, furtive, and the passage of whatever moved up there was more marked by the sound of dripping water.

Ben, standing ready, listening, began to feel strange. As though his body were weightless, he felt as though he were floating. As he stared at the closed door leading into the cabin he could just make out in the growing light of dawn the sharp edges of the frame, the dull shine of the brass knob. But as he stared at them they began to swim in his vision, to expand, to curve and contract. The doorknob bulged out like a balloon and then shrank and became only a pin point of brassy light.

Ben's whole stomach began slowly to move, to roll inside the cavity of his ribs. It rolled up against his diaphragm so that he could hardly breathe, then rolled down, feeling as though it were sucking his heart down.

His knees seemed to become watery and then to tremble. They continued until, with horrible surprise, he heard them slapping against each other, the wet skin making a clear noise.

And yet he felt no fear. He had no desire to run, no desire to put the wrench down and let the man enter, unharmed. He wanted him to come below, to come into the cabin, to stoop and come through the door—and get it.

The sound of the dripping water, the soft sound of the footsteps came slowly, step by step, down the companion ladder.

And then Ben heard the breathing. The sound of it came even through the closed door, and it was the breathing of a man who had just exerted himself greatly. It was slow, deep, almost painful breathing, as though the man were gulping the air.

Ben heard Nick make a tiny noise as he got ready. He heard Penny's breath come out in a soft, low sigh.

THE LION'S PAW

The doorknob made an extremely faint metallic rattle as it was touched on the outside, but for a long time it did not turn, and as Ben stared fixedly at the round, dull shine it began to fade again in his vision. Ben blinked his eyes.

The knob turned slowly but without hesitation. The door swung steadily open, framing a growing rectangle of the gray light of dawn.

A very tall, very thin man stooped and stepped over the threshold.

The trembling of Ben's knees stopped. The roiling of his stomach ended and his vision became clear. He felt cold inside and solid, and his grip on the handle of the wrench was strong as his muscles gathered to bring it crashing down on the man as he was stooped over, one foot in the cabin, the other swinging forward.

Thoughts seemed to flow in a clear, rapid stream through his mind as he began the downward swing of the wrench. "He isn't going to stop us now," Ben thought. "He will not stop us now even if I have to break his head with this wrench and Nick breaks the bones in his legs. We have come too far; we have done too much to be caught now by this stupid jerk. He *will* not stop us."

The wrench was swinging down. In the silence Ben heard a faint hiss of water from Nick's direction, the brushing of cloth from where Penny was standing in the deep shadow.

"Skipper," the man said in a clear, steady voice.

The wrench fell out of Ben's hands. He saw it falling down through the gray light, and it seemed to fall forever, down and down. Then it hit the film of water on the floor with a clean splashing and a dull thump.

Then Ben saw his own arms coming slowly down, his fingers still curved as though gripping something.

"Ben," the man said, his voice louder.

Ben tried to say something, but he could not force the sound past the constriction in his throat. He tried to reach out his hand, but he couldn't move. He could only turn his eyes as he watched the thin arm, the big hand reach toward the bulkhead.

The light blazed on in the cabin.

For an instant Ben saw everything clearly. Nick was crouched under the table, the screw driver back ready to swing. Penny had the hammer far back and was staring at the man's face. Then, fighting with all his might against it, Ben began to cry, and the next thing he knew his face was up against his father's wet shirt, his father was thumping him on the back, his father's arms were tight around his shoulders.

"Skipper," his father said in a low voice. "Skipper."

Ben still couldn't talk and he hated the wet blubbering noise he was making.

Slowly, as Penny realized who it was, she began to cry too. Nick came out from under the table, looked hard at the tall, thin man in a wet khaki uniform patting Ben's back, and waded through the water to stand close beside Penny. When she reached out and took his hand Nick instantly burst into tears.

Finally the man turned Ben loose. He laughed, his voice choked up, and said, "Well—well. I never saw such a warlike scene get so wet so quick. Who were you going to murder?"

He looked at Penny and then at Nick.

"The man," Ben said, still sobbing and trying to stop it. "The thin man." Then Ben said, "Dad."

And he began to cry all over again. In the middle of it he managed to say, "I certainly am ashamed of myself."

Penny pulled on Nick's hand and started out of the cabin. Ben saw them going and grabbed Nick by the shirt. "Don't go," he said. "The blubbering's over. Dad, this is Penny and Nick."

Nick had never seen such a big hand as the one that reached out and took his. But the arm was thin, the skin over the bones so thin he could see the bones moving.

"I've heard a lot about both of you," he said. "From Uncle Pete."

"How'd you find us, Dad?" Ben asked.

"Oh, brother," he said. "When you decide to disappear you do a whacking good job of it. I've been looking for you for a week. Pete swore you were on the east coast; that he had a letter from you in Miami. But when he told me about the wild-goose chase he had gone on to find a black sloop named the *Lion's Paw* I got the first clue. I knew you'd be here. And I've spent all night walking this island."

"The boat's a mess," Ben said.

"Little beat up. What happened?"

"We had to leave. The man went over to check our number and we tried to get out through the Pass. I'd forgotten to secure the dinghy and she smashed through the skylight. Water was up to here."

"You're lucky to get back out of it."

Ben's father looked slowly around the cabin, his eyes seeing everything. When he got to Penny and Nick he smiled. His face was thin, the bones of it showing through, and his gray eyes were big with weariness. "Has Uncle Pete given you a lot of trouble?" he asked.

"Not much. I guess he's been chasing around a lot, but he only got close to us once," Ben said. "But, Dad, where've you been for so long?"

The man sighed. "Long story. Ship went down. Long time in the water. Japs picked me up. Long time on an island. Built a boat. Long time in the boat. Japs got me again—just a long, long time. I'll tell you about it later. Right now I need a bed. Last night just about did me in. Is there anything dry in the boat?"

"The pipe berth forward," Ben said.

"Don't you want something to eat?" Penny asked.

"Thanks, no," he said.

"You're mighty thin, Dad," Ben said anxiously.

"I know a cure for that—and it isn't a handful of rice once a week," he said. "The Japoons never did understand that I'm a man who likes three big meals a day—four, if I can get 'em."

232

"How'd you get here?" Ben asked.

"Came over on the last ferry. And swam the rest of the way." He stopped and looked at them all. "I'm glad to see you," he said slowly; "you're the finest thing I've seen in—how long, Ben?"

"Thirty-one months, Dad," Ben said quietly.

"That long?"

Ben's father put his hand down flat on the table and held himself up. Ben watched him anxiously. "Are you all right, Dad?" he asked.

"Yep. Just shot. A little sleep and I'll be back to battery. And in a week, with some food and some sailing, I'll be able to pull a halyard with any of you. By the way, did you find a Lion's Paw?"

Ben slowly shook his head. "We looked for a long, long time. But we haven't found one."

"We will. We'll go over tomorrow after we've all had a little sack time."

Ben went with his father to the pipe berth forward. When he came back to where Penny and Nick were his eyes were full of tears again, but he didn't cry.

"That's my father," he said quietly. "He came back."

Penny and Nick nodded.

Ben slowly grinned at them. "He—he's——" Then he stopped. After a moment he said in a changed voice, "Let's clean up this mess and then go to bed."

Nick manned the bilge pump while Penny and Ben scrubbed and swabbed, carried all the mattresses and bedding out into the sun, got the stove going to dry out the interior of the boat.

"Your father's very thin," Penny said.

Ben nodded. "I guess the Japanese gave him a rough time. But he doesn't look sick, does he?"

"Not sick. Just thin and sort of worn out," Penny said.

"I want to hear what happened to him," Ben said.

"I do too. I'll bet he's had all sort of adventures."

Ben suddenly laughed. "Wonder where that man is?" he asked. "I wish he'd come back. I want to see him."

"Ummm," Penny said. "But I sort of wish that had been him in the dark. I wanted to hit him."

"I *nearly* hit Dad," Ben said. "If he hadn't said 'Skipper' when he did I would have brained him."

Then they heard the chug-chug of the boat, and soon it came sliding into the bay. The thin man was standing up in it, steering it with his leg.

"Call Nick," Ben whispered. "He ought to hear this."

Penny ran below and came up again with Nick as the man tied his boat up astern and climbed aboard.

The three of them stood beside the cockpit, watching as the man walked toward them. "Howdy," he said.

"Howdy," Nick said.

The man looked at the patched skylight. "Well, I see you tried to git away. Didn't make it, did you?"

"Didn't make it," Nick said.

"Well," the man said, pulling a piece of paper out of his pocket, "I got all the facts. This here boat is rightfully

234

the property of Benjamin R. Sturges, late deceased, and its right name is *Hard A Lee.*" Suddenly he shot out a long bony finger. "And you," he said, "are Ben Sturges, and you two are orphans. And all of you ran away with property that don't belong to you."

The man turned his head a little and spat a stream of tobacco juice onto the deck.

Ben looked down at it, then back up at the man. He had thought that this was going to be funny; that he and Penny and Nick were going to enjoy it. But it wasn't. He felt tired; the man's whiny voice irritated him.

"Get off the boat," Ben said.

"I warned you," the man said. "One more peep out of you and I'll smack you down. . . . Now I've done wired Mr. Lanford to come with the law and git you. And— I'm staying right here until he comes. And—he better bring that five hundred dollars with him, in his pocket."

Ben said, "My father is aboard now. He's asleep and I don't want to bother him. But if you don't get off the boat I'll have to call him."

The man laughed. "I know all about your father. He got kilt in the war." Then the man suddenly reached out and grabbed Ben by the open collar of his shirt and jerked him forward, Ben's feet stumbling over the coaming. With his face about an inch from Ben's he said in a low, mean voice, "So button yer yap before I smack it shut."

Nick and Penny were both moving toward the man, when from the companionway a voice said, "What the devil is going on here?"

THE LION'S PAW

The man turned Ben loose. Ben turned and watched his father come slowly up the companion ladder. He was holding onto the rail with both hands and almost dragging himself up. His face was broken up with weariness and his eyes looked half asleep.

"Who're you?" he asked the man.

"Mister," the man said, "I don't want no trouble out of you. These are runaway kids and there's a reward up for 'em, and I aim to git it. Now just stand where you are, for the law'll be here in a little while."

Ben's father's voice was tired and low as he said, "Get off the boat."

The man took a step toward him. "Who're you, orderin' me off a boat?" he demanded.

"I'm the owner. Get off."

"Mister," the man said, "you look sick and feeble and I'd hate to smack you, but if you don't keep quiet I'm gonna have to."

Ben's father looked down at Ben. "Is this the one?" he asked.

Ben nodded. In the sunlight his father's face looked like ashes and his eyes seemed to have burned holes through the skin. And with his khaki shirt off Ben saw the livid streaks of scars where a whip had been dragged or a rope bound too tightly.

"The owner of this here boat is dead," the man said.

"No," Ben's father said. "He's not dead. He almost was, but he's not. Now, get off."

236

The man began to curse as he walked forward. Ben's father sounded tired and irritated as he said, "Get off the boat, junior. Get off!"

The man was close to him, and because Ben was looking hard at his father he saw the thing start; he saw his father change.

Ben felt strange as he watched it. Before it started Ben would have been able to recognize his father only by the look of his eyes and the way the corners of his mouth curved upward. The rest of him, the tall, thin, weary man, was nothing like his father, who had been big, strong, fast. But when the lank fingers began to curve inward and the elbow moved back the whole man began to change. And when the arm flashed like lightning, the big fist getting blurred in the air, Ben's father was for an instant whole again, his lost weight back on his big bones, the weariness gone, the defeat washed away.

The fist struck the man full in the mouth, coming up, and grated up the thin nose, mashing the nostrils back. As though lifted by wires, the man rose straight up from the deck and, remaining almost horizontal, floated backward, his thin arms and legs dangling in the air, his face carrying a look of amazement and pain.

The man's hips struck the life line, stopping his backward progress, and in slow motion he revolved half around the steel rope, slid off it, and went headfirst into the water, his feet disappearing below the deck.

Ben's father moved back and sat down on the deck-

237

house. "Now I am tired," he said, smiling at them. "Just beat his knuckles with the boat hook if he tries to come on deck again."

Nick stared at Ben's father and then at the place where the man had gone overboard. "Did you see that?" Nick whispered. "He just—flew."

Ben went to the rail and looked down. The man was swimming clumsily toward his boat, climbing headfirst into it, and at last sitting up. Ben let his line go and threw the end of it down on top of him. "Shove off," Ben said. "And don't come back."

As the man's boat drifted away they could hear him yowling and cursing and making huge threats.

Nick went over to stand in front of Ben's father. "What did you hit him with?" Nick asked.

Ben's father laughed. "I feel better," he said. "And a little hungry. How about it, madam?"

"Me?" Penny said.

"I'll cook. I'll cook," Nick said.

"We'll all cook," Ben's father said. "Come on."

They went down the companion ladder and into the main cabin. All the water had been pumped out, but there was still a film of oil over everything, and the deck was littered with junk. Nick's sea shells were scattered all over one half, and Ben's father's over the other half. There were clothes and shoes in soggy lumps, water-logged books and papers, tins of food and charts.

As they started to cross it to the galley Ben's father

238

stopped and held them all back with his outspread arms.

"Look at that," he said, pointing.

On the floor, splashed with oil, was a sea shell the size of Nick's hand. It was yellowish, with orange-and-blue flecks, and on the back of it were the ridges and knobs— the paw of a lion.

Ben and Nick and Penny stared at it.

"Where'd it come from?" Ben asked in a whisper.

Nick went over, squatted down on his haunches, and peered at the shell. "Oh, yes," he said. "I found that one the last day. I just picked it up because it was yellow."

Ben turned slowly and looked at Penny. "You remember?" he asked, his voice low. "He'd come back when we found it."

Penny nodded. "I remember," she said.

Chapter 16

T WAS late at night, and the *Lion's Paw* lay silently at anchor in the little bay. A gentle wind, like an apology for the storm, hummed softly in her rigging; a gentle sea, ashamed of the wreckage it had made, lapped at the smooth hull.

In the main cabin, clean again, Penny and Nick lay—awake.

"Penny," Nick whispered.

"What?"

"Are you awake?"

"Mmmm."

"What's going to happen now?"

Penny turned over on her side so that she could see the blur of his face in the moonlight. "I—don't know, Nick."

"Will he let us stay?"

"He hasn't said anything, has he?"

"No," Nick said. "He hasn't."

"Do you think that—he—doesn't like us?" Penny asked.

"I can't tell," Nick said. "I like him, though, don't you?"

"Yeah," Penny said. After a while she said, "Maybe he'll just want Ben and nobody else."

"Well . . ." Nick said. "If he does, we'll have to go somewhere else."

"Not back to the orphanage, though."

"Not there. We'll just run away again—from here," Nick said.

"Yeah," Penny said. "All over again."

"It won't be like this time, though," Nick said. "There won't be anybody like Ben."

"No. There isn't anybody like Ben."

"I'll hate to do it," Nick said.

"So will I."

"Maybe Ben's father will let us stay until we get rested up good. I got all tired again last night."

"A day or so," Penny said.

"That'll be enough. Where'll we go, Penny?"

"I don't know. Just—away."

"We'll find another boat."

"But not like this one," Penny said.

"It makes me feel sad, thinking about it," Nick said.

"We can come back sometime and visit Ben," Penny said.

"Yeah," Nick said. "Oh, *blast* it!"

Ben's father opened the door of the little cabin and poked his head in. Whispering, he said, "Skipper?"

Ben sat up in bed. "You're the skipper now," he said.

His father came in and sat down on the bed. "Not as sleepy as I thought I was. Just being back on the *Hard A Lee* sets me up."

Ben turned on the light and made more room for his father. "Did they—were they pretty rough?" he asked.

"Not too bad. . . . Ben, what about Penny and Nick?"

"How do you mean?"

"Do you like 'em?"

Ben waited a long time and then he said, "Yeah. I like 'em almost as much as I do you, Dad."

"Are they that good?"

Ben nodded. "They're all right, Dad."

"I went around to the orphanage and calmed them down a little. I can adopt them if you think you'd like it."

"I would," Ben said.

"They look like pretty good shipmates to me."

Ben sat forward. "You wait until you know them better. They're—they're all right."

"Okay. As soon as I get myself squared away with the Navy I'll adopt them."

Ben swung his legs out of the bed. "Can I tell 'em? Now?"

His father grinned. "If you think it's worth waking them up about."

"They won't mind," Ben said, climbing out of bed.

He opened the door to the main cabin and whispered, "Nick?"

"What?" Nick said instantly.

"You sleep?"

"I don't think so," Nick said.

"Is Penny?"

"No," Penny said.

"Well, then," Ben said, "how would you like to be adopted by my dad?"

For a long moment there was nothing but silence in the cabin. Then Penny began to cry softly, her face in the pillow.

"Don't mind her," Nick said, jumping out of bed. "Is he going to do it, Ben? Is he?"

"If you want to," Ben said.

"I don't know about her, but I do," Nick said.

Wailing, Penny said, "I—do—too."

Fisheating River

na River

Peace Creek

Charlotte
Harbor □

Charlotte
Harbor

acida

sparilla
ound

sparilla Island

Locosia I.

Pine
Island
Sound

Captiva I.

Sanibel I.

Gulf of Mexico

□ Punta
Gorda

Cula □

□ Buckingham

□ Fort Myers

Caloosahatchee River

Big Cypress Swamp